Ridin' with the Pack

Also by the Authors

Yakima Henry Series

Peter Brandvold

The Peacemaker's Tale Series

Kathleen O'Neal Gear

Saga of the Mountain Sage Series

W. Michael Gear

Levi Johnson Mountain Man Scout Series

Ash Lingam

Bullets Trilogy

Nicholas Osborn

Hell West of the Pecos

V.J. Rose

Dunbar Series

John D. Nesbitt

Praise for the Authors

"No one reads a Gear novel without being transformed in beautiful ways."

— *True West Magazine*

"John Nesbitt knows working cowboys and ranch life well enough for you to chew the dirt with his characters as this tale unfolds."

— *True West*

"In the realm of slam-bang-action writing about the Old West, the rest of us can't hold a candle to Peter Brandvold."

— J. Lee Butts, author of *And Kill Them All*

Ridin' with the Pack

Volume Three

Peter Brandvold   V.J. Rose   W. Michael Gear

Kathleen O'Neal Gear   Nicholas Osborn

John D. Nesbitt   Ash Lingam

WOLFPACK
PUBLISHING
— EST 2013 —

Ridin' with the Pack: Volume Three
Paperback Edition
Copyright © 2025 by the Individual Authors:
Peter Brandvold, Nicholas Osborn, Kathleen O'Neal Gear, Ash Lingam,
V.J. Rose, W. Michael Gear, and John D. Nesbitt

Wolfpack Publishing
1707 E. Diana Street
Tampa, FL 33610

www.wolfpackpublishing.com

Paperback ISBN 979-8-89567-315-7
Ebook ISBN 979-8-89567-314-0

Contents

Foreword

Dear Reader,

Welcome to our newest anthology of Western fiction—a collection that gathers together some of the most compelling short stories we've published. This volume doesn't just celebrate the spirit of the West in the abstract; it showcases it through seven vivid tales that will carry you from rugged mountains and windswept plains to shadowed saloons and lonely trails. Each story in this collection offers a distinct perspective on the frontier, and together they form a tapestry of adventure, justice, and survival.

In "Black on Black," you'll meet Marshal One-Eyed Jack Black, a figure both feared and respected, whose pursuit of justice leads him deep into the heart of a lawless town. "Dead Hand" takes a more haunting turn, spinning a tale of greed, gold, and the spectral consequences of a gambler's final bet. "Little Snake" follows a young man navigating the unforgiving canyons along the Little Snake River, where every choice could mean life or death.

The pace quickens in "One Shot," where a seasoned gunfighter is forced to decide whether one final bullet can make a difference. "Shadrach" explores themes of betrayal and redemption as an outlaw confronts the past he can no longer outrun. "Woman With No Eyes" adds a touch of eerie mysticism to the collection, weaving a story of a mysterious stranger whose presence changes an entire community. Finally, "Wrong Side of a Bullet" reminds us how thin the line can be between right and wrong when a fateful trigger pull determines a man's destiny.

At Wolfpack Publishing, our mission has always been to honor the legacy of Western storytelling while discovering fresh voices who can bring new life to the genre. These stories do exactly that. They balance classic motifs of heroism, frontier justice, and the stark beauty of the land, with unique twists that keep the genre evolving. I'm grateful to each of the authors in this collection for their craftsmanship and passion; their contributions make this anthology an unforgettable ride.

So, whether you're a longtime fan of Westerns or new to the genre, I invite you to settle in, turn the page, and let these stories take you westward. You'll encounter gunslingers, outlaws, and lawmen, and landscapes that feel both timeless and alive. Thank you for joining us on this journey. The trail awaits!

Jake Bray
Editor
President, Wolfpack Publishing

Ridin' with the Pack

One Shot

A Short Story

By Peter Brandvold

One Shot

Yakima Henry sat back in the shadows of Rattlesnake Ridge's only watering hole, near a wood stove wearing a bullet crease in its left front door.

A fire snapped quietly in the stove, making the big, black coffee pot on its warming rack chug softly, slowly.

Outside the wind howled, blowing up dust on the wide main street lined with mostly abandoned shops, and lacing the late-summer air with an autumnal chill.

Yakima turned his half-empty beer mug around in its own circle of condensed moisture on the age-grayed table scarred by the knives of many men who'd wanted to leave their marks with their own initials over the past twenty, thirty years. Buffalo hunters, men who'd trailed the great cattle herds up from Texas...

As if that would save them from where they were all headed, the only thing they all had in common.

Yakima smiled.

He stared down at his rough-skinned hand at the base of the mug and wondered how many of the initials still had men to go with them. How many didn't? How many had been carved by men, some drifters like himself, out of some unconscious urge to live forever—or for as long as the table lasted—here on these battered, old cotton-wood planks in a nameless saloon in this former hide hunter's camp on the parched plains of western Kansas—Rattlesnake Ridge.

Middle of goddamn nowhere.

But then, that's where Yakima was from. It was where he'd die.

And why not? He was most at home there.

Here.

Nowhere.

Outside, tied to the hitchrack under the branch ramada sloping away from the adobe brick, tin-roofed hovel, Wolf didn't like the newcomers. As the three men rode past him from behind, the black stallion with one white front sock, pinned his ears back, shook his head, and arched his tail. Pulling at the reins looped around the worn cottonwood rack, he curveted to get a look at them.

They were three rough men with crow-like features in dusty trail gear not unlike Yakima's own battered hat, calico shirt, neck-knotted bandanna held together with dust and sweat, and denim trousers badly faded and worn nearly white on the insides of his thighs, where his legs hugged the saddle.

Itinerant men. Drifters. Six-shooters strapped to their waists, rifles bristling in saddle boots.

Outlaws.

Killers.

As they rode around Wolf and put their horses up to the hitchrack, Yakima lowered his impassive gaze again to his hand still turning the beer mug in the circle of water that had run down from the sides of the glass. His doe-skin gloves lay one atop the other, to the right of the glass. A wood-handled Arkansas toothpick sat to its left, atop three age-brittled wanted circulars.

He'd unsheathed the knife to sharpen it on his whetstone.

He had no interest in carving initials. He never had. He couldn't understand the urge. All men died. If it was only initials you left behind in a dried-out, ancient, mostly abandoned place like Rattlesnake Ridge in which graves far outnumbered the living surrounded by only rock and sage for as far as the eye could see, then you'd never lived in the first place.

The hell with you.

Yakima was alive. He had the scars from knives and bullets to prove it.

He had a lone grave in Arizona he visited every few years to remind him.

The name sketched into the stone slab he'd used for a marker. Her marker.

Faith...

Gone these many years. There would be no other.

A warm breeze blew through the batwing doors. It kicked up dust on the street behind Wolf and the newcomers' horses. It smelled like sage, leather, and horses.

It caressed Yakima's severely chiseled face—the face of a Cheyenne mixed with the German of his prospector father. Both dead long ago, his parents. The Deutsch showed only in his lens-clear green eyes framed and contrasted to startling effect by straight, black hair hanging to his broad shoulders sculpted by years of horsemanship and hard toil.

A stag-horned .44 Colt was thonged low on his right thigh, gunslinger style.

The beaded leather sheath for the knife lay behind it, strapped to his cartridge belt, the leather loops filled with .44 brass.

"You don't like me, do you?" came a man's voice from

out on the covered boardwalk fronting the earthen-floored saloon.

Yakima saw one of the three men bent forward talking to Wolf who stood back away from the man, glaring at him, front hooves spread.

The man leaned forward at the waist, fists on his hips, two pistols tied to his thighs over his dusty denims. He jutted his chin forward like a wedge. "No, you don't like me one bit! What is it, hoss? Is it my *smell*?" He lifted each arm in turn, sniffing. "Can't be me. I had a bath only last Christmas. I don't like *your* smell!"

Wolf drew his head up, biting his bit, angry-bright eyes lowered, white rings above them. He whickered, pawed the ground angrily with one front hoof.

The man teasing him laughed with the other two then they removed their hats and swatted them against their legs as they headed for the batwings, dust wafting around them. They pushed through the louvre doors and headed for the long, plankboard bar on their right, ahead and on Yakima's left. A mirror stretched behind it, above a counter cluttered with glasses and bottles. A pot simmered on a small, black range, steam rising around its lid.

"He don't like you, Casey," said one of the other men —tall and dark and wearing a battered, ancient Confederate cavalry kepi. "He don't like you a bit. Maybe you oughta take that bath on the Fourth of July, too, not just at Christmas!"

"How 'bout I take one only once every *two years*, like you, Frank!" Casey said as he set his arms atop the bar and looked at the apron standing on the other side of it, giving them each a dark look as he pensively, apprehensively twisted an upswept end of his groomed mustache.

Frank Starrett and the third man, Albert Driscoll, laughed. Len Casey, the man who'd been teasing Wolf, glowered at them both and told the barman clad in a striped, collarless shirt and string tie, "A bottle an' three glasses."

He slapped the bar. The apron jumped with a start, glared at the man, and reached under the bar for a bottle. He pulled three shot glasses off a pyramid, popped the cork from the bottle, and filled each glass. He corked the bottle and left it on the bar. He stepped back and shuttled a glance at Yakima sitting back in the unnamed saloon's rear shadows.

Yakima met the man's eyes and smiled.

He said, "I'll have what they're having."

"You sure you better?" asked the barman.

The three newcomers, the only other men in the room, looked over at Yakima.

"Might add to the beer," Yakima said, his smile in place, taking the edge off his insult. His gaze went to the three men bellied up to the bar.

Casey had a hound-dog look. Tall and bony with a potbelly and a shriveled-up ear under his funnel-brimmed hat. The ear was a red knot showing beneath his hat. An identifying mark, for sure.

The screams of the girl rose in Yakima's ears. In his mind's eye, he saw her dragged out of the saloon on the outskirts of Pawnee, blond hair flying about her head and shoulders left bare by her low-cut, metallic green dress edged with black lace.

Through blood dribbling into the half-breed's right eye as he lay on the boardwalk, groaning, making several feeble attempts to rise, he grimaced and ground his jaws in anger when he saw what Casey, his pants down around his ankles, was doing to the wailing girl. He bent her forward over a wooden well cover in the street's center.

There was screaming and shouting, the whinnying of

horses, the barking of dogs, and the ground-shuddering thunder of pistols and rifles from inside the bank behind Yakima and from out on the street where the townsmen were trying to keep their money right where they'd left it for safekeeping.

Their hard-earned cash.

Life savings.

Money enough to get them through another month during a dry year of parched crops, porridge meals, and cattle showing their ribs...

Albert Driscoll was short and stout with a long, tangled beard. He walked with a slight limp from a bullet a drunk whore had shot through his knee in Mesilla.

In Yakima's mind, he saw Driscoll haze the bank manager out of the bank's front door and onto the boardwalk, push the suited, gray-headed man to his knees, and shoot him in the back of the head.

Pop!

Just like that.

The report of Driscoll's .44 was so real in the half-breed's memory—it had happened three weeks ago—he felt himself jerked with a start at it now.

The tall, dark Starrett, standing beside Driscoll and rolling a quirley with his hands up close to his umber-colored, wool vest inside his broadcloth jacket, had run out of the bank whooping and hollering, bulging saddle-bags draped over his shoulder, pausing on the boardwalk to shoot a man crawling toward him, a cocked revolver in the man's hand.

Starrett drilled him through the forehead.

The man had dropped his head instantly and rolled onto his back so that the town marshal's badge pinned to his brown leather vest glinted in the afternoon sunshine. The marshal's beefy, younger deputy lay dead in the street behind him—both shot in their offices before the gang of seven had started marauding, three robbing the bank, three robbing the saloon from which they'd taken the girl, whose screams still echoed in Yakima's head as the barman brought him a shot of whiskey and set it on the table before him.

"Sure you oughta?" the apron said, stitching his brows together. "I don't want no trouble in here."

He hooked a thumb over his shoulder to indicate a placard nailed to a square-hewn ceiling support post on which had been written in large, blocky letters:

INJUNS SHALL NOT BE SERVED
HALF BREEDS SERVED ONLY BEER
JUST ONE!!
NO HARD LIQUOR

Yakima smiled at the apron as he picked up the shot.

"Here's to ya," he said, and dumped the whiskey into his beer.

He plucked a dime off the table before him, flipped it in the air. The barman tried to catch it, missed, and stooped with a curse and a glare at the half-breed to pluck it out of the dirt at his feet.

"Injuns drinkin' whiskey, now," said Driscoll as the apron made his way back along the bar. "What kind of a place is this, anyway?"

"Sure as hell not a family place," said Casey, and threw back his shot.

He refilled his glass from the bottle on the bar.

As Casey had galloped out of town with the others, their dust churning and a wounded horse screaming, Casey had jerked the pantiless whore up off the well and swung her onto the back of his horse. He'd shot a man running toward him shouting and wielding a double-barrel shotgun, then, as the man crumpled and fired the gut-shredder skyward, slapped his steeldust with his rein-ends. He'd disappeared into the thick cloud of dust trailing the six others in the gang.

Three dogs had chased him, barking.

His whooping and hollering and the rataplan of his galloping horse's hooves dwindled behind him until there was only the screams and wails of several townsmen dying on the street.

Casey looked at Yakima over his shoulder.

"Say, that's a helluva gash you got on your head," he said, frowning, a big Russian bristling from the cross-draw holster on his left hip, the walnut grips angled over his belly. "How'd you get it?"

Yakima smiled. "Cut myself shavin'."

———

CASEY FROWNED and looked at Starrett and Driscoll standing to either side of him.

Frank Starrett turned and shot Yakima a flinty, dark-eyed look.

The half-breed glanced down at the three wanted dodgers lying under his gloves.

Poking up above the gloves were the words:

WANTED
DEAD OR ALIVE
$1000 REWARD

Striding slowly toward Yakima, thumbs hooked behind his crossed, double cartridge belts, Starrett said, "You a smart ass...breed?"

Yakima broadened his grin but said nothing.

Starrett stopped. He stared at Yakima.

The half-breed had his hand on his right thigh, just

above his holstered, stag-gripped Colt. His trigger finger twitched as he dug it into his leg, through his buckskin pants. He was ready.

Take another step, he silently urged the man before him. He was still smiling but a darkness had entered his eyes.

Time to get business out of the way and think about holing up somewhere for the night. Somewhere out of town. By a spring—he'd seen his way into town, knowing these three had been heading here to Rattlesnake Ridge, there not being another town out here for them to head to. He'd swung wide around them and gotten ahead of them.

"Go ahead," he said.

Hoof thuds and the clatter of wagon wheels sounded from outside. Starrett turned his head to look out the window right of the batwing doors.

Yakima did the same but kept an eye on the outlaw before him and on the other two standing at the bar and who were also looking outside at the newcomers.

A wagon was pulling up in front of the unnamed saloon. A young woman wearing a brown Stetson was driving. She stopped the sorrel with a light pull on the reins and, when the wagon had stopped, she set the wagon brake, turned to say something to the old man sitting on the wooden seat beside her. He said nothing, just kept looking straight ahead.

He was Indian. There was no mistaking that. Long, blue-gray hair tumbled down from his black, badly weathered felt hat. His face was a weathered ruin. He wore a calico shirt under a striped blanket coat, denim trousers, and high-topped moccasins, their tops rolled down, decorated with dyed porcupine quills.

The woman appeared very young, still a girl in her late teens. She was not Indian, making them an odd pair. She wrapped the sorrel's reins around the brake handle then stepped down from the driver's box, walked around the rear of the wagon which had several sacks of dry goods and canned goods stacked in the box, and moved up beside the old man. She held her hands up to him. He shook his head and, pulling his striped blanket coat closer around him against the cold, stepped down onto the wagon's right front wheel, then, holding the small bar running along the side of the seat above him, stepped gingerly down to the ground.

The girl had thick brown hair and a nice figure snugged into the brown plaid mackinaw and black wool skirt she wore—spoke to the old man, hooked an arm around his, and led him up the two steps to the boardwalk fronting the saloon, under the ramada. She held him tightly by his right arm as she led him—he had a shuffling gate, as though he had little feeling in his feet, or maybe his legs were arthritic, or both—across the boardwalk and through the batwings.

Starrett and his partners were distracted by the old man and the girl.

She owned an almost overpowering beauty, silver rings dangling from her ears, inside her thick, brown hair. As struck as much by the girl as the other males in the room, Yakima slackened the hand on his thigh and mentally cursed. He'd had an opportunity to deliver justice for the folks in Pawnee and to earn a stake for himself and the stallion before innocents save the barman had been present.

Now it had slipped away.

In his mind's eye, the face of the whore appeared as he'd found her, lying in a patch of sage, clothes in only a few strips of her dress and camisole, her legs and feet pale and bare. A fly buzzed around her mouth, lighted on her lower lip.

She'd been blue and swollen; she'd been lying there,

animals having gotten to her, for days while Yakima had been holed up in the Pawnee doctor's spare bedroom, recovering from the graze he'd taken to his head from a ricochet during the chaos of the robbery, and while he'd been hunting the other three robbers who'd split up from the men before him now...and who wouldn't be alive much longer...enjoying their booze...their women... looking forward to meeting up with the other three robbers after they'd taken time to cool their heels and avoid any shadowers like the inept posse that had gone out after them only to end up as the whore had--dead in the sage, some of their horses shot out from under them.

Frank Starrett, Len Casey, and Albert Driscoll wouldn't be meeting up with the other three, as all six had planned. Having tracked them all, taking one group down, Yakima had savied what they'd been up to.

They weren't the first savages he'd tracked.

And they wouldn't be splitting the money.

Yakima had the bank loot in his own saddlebags draped over the back of the chair across the table from him, some of the coins and greenbacks splattered with Kilroy, Mahoney, and Dick Blaze's blood. His prized Winchester Yellowboy repeater leaned against the chair— a silent, steel sentinel and protector of the half-breed's plunder.

The six highwaymen were worth a thousand dollars each in reward money, extra for the loot. More for the dead banker.

When he'd taken these three down, making his haul a full six, he'd have a nice stake to take him to Arizona, where he'd put wildflowers on his dead lover's grave and then drift...always drifting...without Faith...farther south into old Mexico where he'd spend the winter frolicking with the dusky-skinned senoritas on the sandy, palm-lined beaches along the Sea of Cortez.

Faith wouldn't begrudge him.

She'd want him to be a man. A man needed a woman now and then even if they weren't and never would be Faith...

———

THE GIRL STOPPED with the old man just inside the batwing doors that clattered shut behind them.

Her tan eyes swept the room beneath her brown hat, finding Yakima, lingering on him, the knife on the table beside his beer mug. She looked at the rifle and the saddlebags across from the big, dark, green-eyed man in buckskins. She was careful, this girl. Protective.

She slid her probing, vaguely apprehensive gaze to the three men who'd turned toward her, their backs to the bar. They stared at her flatly, expressionless. Yes, they stared without expression, but Yakima knew the lack of expression belied what they were feeling, because he felt the male tug himself though he tried to deny it.

But he was a man as they were men. Different in many ways, thank God, but he was a man. A girl like that, with those lens-clear, smoldering eyes, could burrow into a man's guts and twist them.

The barman looked at her from behind the bar. "The same?"

The girl looked at him, nodded, and held up one gloved finger. "Uno."

Her voice chimed beguilingly. Spanish. She was Mexican or had Mexican blood. Yakima saw it now in her brown eyes, in the thick, dark hair, the olive tone of her skin.

"Comin' up," the barman said with a wry smile. He set a goblet on the bar and splashed whiskey into it. "One shot."

Yakima could see that there was more than one shot in the glass.

The apron came around from behind the bar and set the glass on the table nearest the doors.

He looked at the girl who was helping the old man to the table, moving very slowly beside him, letting him take his time.

"One shot," the barman said.

He walked to the stove near Yakima, picked up a leather swatch and a white stone mug from a low table beside it. He filled the cup with the hot, smoking brew and set it on the table on which he'd set the whiskey.

"One shot," he said, smiling and shaking his head as he walked around behind the bar and gave the stewpot a stir.

The girl got the old man seated at the table, gave a little grunt as, using her knee, she slid the chair forward. She walked around the table and sat in the chair at the other end of it and before which sat the steaming mug of coffee.

The old man sat with his hands resting on his thighs, looking down at the half-filled goblet before him. His eyes were flat, implacable. But he was anticipating that first sip, Yakima knew, as he did himself after a long drift. The old man probably didn't get to town all that much. Yakima guessed he and the girl lived around here somewhere, maybe on a little rattlesnake ranch or at a stage relay station. There was an obvious bond between them that had made Yakima figure they lived together.

She was devoted to him.

Her grandfather?

There was no familial resemblance, and she didn't appear to have any Indian blood mixed with Mexican. Sometimes…often, in fact…it was hard to tell. Odd what features came out when the two races mixed. Something in the sharpness of the old man's features, the fierce, broad nose, the close-set, implacable eyes; his leanness, the long, once-strong legs of a natural horseman, told Yakima he might be Arapaho.

An old fighter born with the bark on, a war chief with many dead soldiers notched on his war shield.

His people were gone. He was alone.

With the girl.

She loved him. There was no doubt.

Yakima sipped his beer and whiskey. He looked at the three outlaws at the bar.

Starrett was staring at him in the backbar mirror. When Yakima locked eyes with him, the man averted his gaze to his drink.

The other two were murmuring among themselves. Starrett was preoccupied with the half-breed, occasionally stealing looks at the girl who leaned forward, arms on the table before her, hands around the mug as though to warm them through her gloves, taking occasional, tentative sips of the hot brew.

Outside, Wolf whinnied.

Yakima turned to see the horse looking to his right.

Footsteps sounded, spurs changing, beneath the howling wind that was blowing up dust and bouncing tumbleweeds along the street to the south. A man-shaped shadow passed the dirty window to the left of the batwings. The newcomer stopped before the door, peered inside, blue eyes sweeping the room quickly, cautiously, his gaze pausing briefly on Yakima, the big half-breed being always a figure of interest, then pushed inside.

The batwings clattered back into place behind him as he moved to the bar, shaking his head topped with a high-crowned cream Stetson. "Boy, it sure is blowin' its lungs out out there! Ain't seen the like in a while." He slapped his hand on the bar and looked at the barman. "Whiskey, if you will, Jake."

Yakima looked at the man in the backbar mirror. A five-pointed star was pinned to his black wool vest inside his canvas jacket.

"Comin' right up, Marshal."

As the barman filled a shot glass, the lawman looked out the window left of the batwings, gave his head another fateful wag. "When it blows like this it's gonna keep blowin'. Likely get some rain out of it." He lifted his chin, sniffed. "Smell that? Rain. That's a storm comin' sure as the Lutheran women giggle over the communion wine in the church basement after services!"

He slapped the bar and roared.

He turned to the girl and the old Indian and said loudly, "What do you think of this weather, Dark Moon? We got a storm comin'?"

The old man nodded and stared into his whiskey which he'd taken a couple of sips of, savoring each before swallowing then setting the glass back down very carefully, using both his red, gnarled, arthritic hands very carefully. He spoke to the girl in a language Yakima recognized as a dialect of the Arapaho tribe. He turned his head to peer out the window to his right, spoke again to the girl, raising his right hand and looking up as though at the sky, and fell silent.

Carefully, he raised the shot glass and took another slow sip.

The girl hooked her left arm around the chair back and looked at the barman. "The old one says for me to stable Rio and the wagon. The storm will strike soon. The washes will be *inundado*." She held up a hand and opened it. "Especially for an old horse like Rio."

The barman glanced up the stone stairs with a knotted pole railing rising along the saloon's rear wall to a second story. "You and Dark Moon take the first room on the left. Mrs. Ravencoat scrubbed it just this mornin', put clean blankets on the beds."

"Thank you, senor," she said with a haunting smile.

She sipped her coffee, leaned toward Dark Moon, and spoke a few words in what sounded to Yakima like fluent Arapaho, then slid her chair back and rose. At the bar, the lawman threw his whiskey back and set down the shot glass. Running his jacket sleeve across his mouth, he pulled his hat brim down low on his forehead and walked toward the blowing batwings.

"Let me help you with that, Isabel!"

———

YAKIMA PONDERED HIS OPTIONS.

You didn't argue with an old Indian about the weather. You'd drown in a flooded wash every time. Besides, the three outlaws were still here, playing poker at a table near the bar now, their half-empty whiskey bottle on the table before them. They'd likely be spending the night.

So would Yakima.

He didn't want to try and take them down in here. That lawman, though he had to be pushing sixty, might try to arrest him. Half-Breeds who took down White men, even outlaw White men, were frowned upon. Yakima had been locked up enough times for that very thing, even when he'd had good reason, to know he didn't like the experience.

He'd also killed enough lawmen in his time—they'd all needed it—to know that wasn't a favorable experience, either. He didn't want to kill the old town marshal of Rattlesnake Ridge. He didn't want to butt horns with him, either. He didn't want a fight. He just wanted to avenge the dead folks the gang had left back on the main street of Pawnee and collect his reward money.

He'd turn the bodies in—including the three he'd left in a cave about fifteen miles south of Rattlesnake Ridge—to the sitting lawman at Pawnee. The man—no doubt the entire town—would be happy to see them. They'd be happy to see the money, too.

The town marshal and the girl returned to the saloon.

Both were peppered with grit from the blowing wind, the girl's hair forming a tumbleweed about her lovely head. Both slapped their hats against their legs, making dust waft. The girl returned to her seat across from the old Indian, Dark Moon, who had only about a quarter inch of whiskey remaining in his glass.

The lawman walked up to the bar, said, "Hit me again, Jake. One more time. Just one more. If Millie smells it on my breath, I'll be sleepin' with the dogs in the stable again!"

He and the barman chuckled.

"Just one," the barman said, setting a freshly filled shot glass down on the bar before the marshal. He looked at the old Indian and then, conspiratorially at Starrett and the other two outlaws playing poker, and said, "Just one more!"

He laughed.

"Uno," said Albert Driscoll, glancing at the girl, who sat with her back to the bar, over his left shoulder.

"Si," said the barman. "Uno!"

"Say," the lawman said, turning to the three outlaws standing to his right, "where you fellas from?"

Don't, Yakima silently warned the man. *Don't do that. Millie's waiting for you.*

"Who—us?" asked Frank Starrett, leaning forward to see across Casey.

Looking a little picked upon, Len Casey said, "What about him?"

He jerked his chin to indicate Yakima.

"I'll get to him," the lawman said, placing his left elbow on the edge of the bar as he turned to face the three outlaws. "Who're you? Where you from?"

In the backbar mirror, Yakima saw the old man smile amiably.

The girl, Isabel, turned around in her chair to glance at the lawman and the outlaws at the bar. Then she turned back forward in her chair.

Len Casey turned to look at Starrett.

Starrett shook his head slightly, looked across Starrett at the lawman, and smiled.

"I'm Wayne Honeycutt from Sioux City, Iowa." Placing his hand on Casey's shoulder, he said, "This here is Clancy Hale from Belle Fourche and that ugly little drink o' water is Web Brewster from Nacogdoches."

"Where you workin'?"

"Nowhere at the moment," said Starrett. "Say, you don't know any ranch currently hirin', do you?"

The lawman grimaced and shook his head. "Nah, nah. Sorry. Getting' purty late in the year, don't ya know? I heard the stage line might be lookin' for a shotgun messenger, but just one."

Again, he shook his head.

The lawman sipped his whiskey and turned full around to face Yakima.

"What about you?"

"I'm Billy Wild from the Black Hills."

He'd once spent two days in jail with a Billy Wild, whose nose he'd broken in a saloon fight in Lac Cruces."

"Billy Wild, Billy Wild," the lawman said, stitching his brows together and nodding, pensive. He was likely riffling through the wanted circulars in his mind.

Damn, Yakima thought. *I sure hope Billy doesn't have any paper on him...*

Yakima looked at the girl. She was staring at him.

She blinked once, slowly, and looked at Starrett. He looked down.

The girl turned away.

"Huh," the lawman said, finally. He smiled, old gray eyes showing a sly shrewdness. "You sure don't look like any Billy Wild, but..."

He turned, picked up his shot glass, threw the rest of his whiskey back, set the glass back down on the bar, and said, "Well, been nice palaverin'. Hope you gents enjoy your time in our fair city." He chuckled and leaned toward Len Casey standing to his right and added, "Ain't much of a city anymore, but it sure stomped with its tail up back in the day!"

He chuckled and turned to the barman who'd dipped up some stew and was eating it, a checked napkin tucked into his shirt collar.

"Thanks for the drink, Jake!"

"Anytime, Marshal!"

"Dark Moon, Isabel," he said, and tapped two fingers to his hat brim as he headed toward the batwings blowing back and forth in the wind.

He pushed out through the doors, swung left, and, holding his hat down tight on his head, strode away.

Frank Starrett looked at Yakima in the backbar mirror, gave a coyote smile, and said, "Billy Wild, huh?"

Yakima returned the man's smile. "Nice to meet ya, Wayne Honeycutt."

———

YAKIMA FINISHED his beer and whiskey and heaved himself out of his chair with a groan.

Damn, he'd gotten comfortable.

Old age was setting in. But then, he wondered how many miles he'd ridden in his life, across one side of the frontier to the other and back again...as far north as Churchill, Canada, hunting a man...deep into the Chiricahuas in southeast Arizona and farther south...deep in the Sierra Madre while prospecting with a one-eyed old desert rat named Kilarney Masters.

They'd found enough gold for a basketed bottle of baconora and some fat whores. Much to their chagrin, they'd also found a war party led by the mad warrior Moon Face. They'd left Mexico shooting. What else was new? It was Mexico.

He'd always left it shooting.

He smiled.

All in all, it hadn't been a bad life.

But one without Faith for these past eight years. That part made him fight the wolves away from his campfires with a little less vigor. For Wolf, he fought them, mostly. When Wolf was gone, he'd invite them in. It'd be time.

Long enough without her.

He couldn't live without his woman *and* his horse.

He draped the saddlebags over his left shoulder, holding the Yellowboy with the same hand atop the same shoulder. He walked to the bar, set his empty mug down.

"Another beer and another shot of that tarantula juice. I'll be damned if it don't grow on a feller. Might as well pour it into the beer. Why dirty another glass?"

He smiled.

"Hey!" objected Len Casey. "See the sign?"

"Savage no read!"

Yakima pulled his right fist back behind his shoulder and thrust it forward with a force that came all the way up from his heels. The clenched, red maul smashed into

Casey's face with a wet, crunching *smack!*, making the man's nose explode like a ripe tomato.

The man yelped.

He fell against Starrett then dropped to the floor, glaring up at Yakima with fury in his eyes to either side of his nose that resembled a pile of freshly ground, bloody beef. He swept his right hand to the grips of the .44 holstered on his right thigh but forestalled the movement when Yakima brought the Yellowboy down off his shoulder, cocked it one-handed, planted his left foot against the man's chest, shoving him down, and aimed the Winchester at the bloody face from six inches away.

Casey glared up at him, fear nudging away his fury.

His lower jaw sagged.

Yakima lifted his flinty-eyed gaze to Starrett and Driscoll standing behind him.

Both men had their hands on their holstered guns. Frozen in place. Hard eyes on the half-breed.

At Yakima's feet, Casey groaned hollowly through the hands cupped to his nose.

"He broke it," he lamented. "Oh, goddamn...he *broke* it!"

Yakima kept his eyes on Driscoll and Casey. They stared back at him, shuttling their gazes between the Yellowboy and his eyes, wondering, *How fast could he bring it up*?

Yakima's finger drew taut against the Winchester's trigger.

He could finish Casey and drill the other two before either got his gun out.

Why not?

He slid his eyes just far enough to the right that he could see the girl turned in her chair, watching him, eyes wide, bright with expectation.

The old man stared at him over his empty goblet.

He could do it, Yakima thought, returning his gaze to the three men before him.

The girl and the old man were out of the way.

Still, there was a chance of a ricochet.

Let Starrett decide.

He said as much with his eyes.

Starrett and Driscoll stared at the Yellowboy angled down at the face of Len Casey.

"Uh-uh," Casey said through the hands cupped over his nose, staring into that round, steel maw—the large dark eye of a malevolent god. "Don't do it."

Starrett turned his head to share a glance with Driscoll in the back bar mirror.

Both men removed their hands from their guns.

The barman lifted his head to peer warily down at Casey on the floor beneath the half-breed's boot. "Uh, let me, uh..." he said, glancing at Yakima, "let me get that drink for ya, mister!"

He hurried away to pour the beer.

Yakima depressed the Yellowboy's hammer and glanced at the barman filling a fresh mug with sudsy beer. "Set it on my table with a bowl of that stew. I'll be back."

He walked backward toward the blowing batwings over and through which the wind howled like a tormented demon. He kept the Yellowboy aimed at the outlaws. He passed the girl and the old man and stopped in front of the batwings. He looked at the nervous apron.

"Bring Dark Moon another one, too." He smiled at the girl, at the old man. "What the hell? You're in town. Live a little."

They smiled back at him.

He backed through the batwings, tossed the saddlebags over Wolf's back, on top of the bags already in place behind the saddle, and shoved his rifle into its scabbard.

He stepped into the saddle and turned the stallion toward the stable.

———

IN A REAR STALL, the black drew water from the wooden bucket Yakima had set in front of him.

When he'd finished with the water, the horse returned to work on the parched corn the half-breed had poured out for him in a wooden trough. Yakima ran a brush over the horse's back, plucking out bits of grass and burs. He went to work on the coarse black tail, giving it the same slow, thorough care.

The horse was Yakima's only friend.

The crunching sounds of the chewing stallion, the howling wind, the occasional snorts of Reno in the next stall, and the creaking of the stable's vertical timbers against the gale were the only sounds. Light angling through the gaps between the timbers was fading quickly as the windy dusk settled in.

Yakima ran the brush through the tip of the tail, removing dust and grit, pulling out bits of sage, grease-wood, and tumbleweed. Outside, a spur chinged faintly. Yakima heard it beneath the screeching wind that, when he'd ridden over from the unnamed saloon, had been threaded with the first few icy drops of rain. Now he could hear it pelting lightly against the stable.

Gravel ground beneath a boot.

Again, faintly. But the half-breed hadn't gotten as old as he was with poor hearing.

He turned to the front of the stable dark save for the murky light angling between the vertical timbers. The two big doors were closed. Shifting movement outside interrupted the light angling through them. Shadows moved in the gap beneath them. Wolf lifted his head from the trough, turned to the door, and whickered.

"Shh." Yakima patted the horse's back. "Stay, boy."

He set the brush down, opened the stall door, and stepped into the alley.

He closed the stall door and moved quietly down the straw-strewn alley toward the front. As he did, Rio poked his head over the low door of his stall and gave an inquiring snort.

"Shh."

Yakima patted horse's snout as he passed and continued forward, unsnapping the keeper thong from over his .44 holstered low on his right thigh. When he was ten feet from the doors, he saw the shadows under the door were no longer moving. Shadows showing through the gaps between the timbers were no longer moving, either.

Starrett and his men were just outside, waiting.

The wind howled. The timbers creaked.

The rain pelted the stable, a softer sound than the sand, nearly drowned by the wind's banshee wails.

Yakima slid the Colt from its holster, held it straight down against his right leg.

He squeezed the staghorn handles.

Time to grow that steak, head to Faith…continue without her to Mexico.

Always without her.

Both doors jerked open.

Three men lurched between them, hatted shadows against the near-dark sky behind them. The lazy light glinted off gun barrels.

"Die, you dirt-worshipping, half-breed cur!"

Yakima's Colt crashed once, twice, three times as two of the outlaws' wayward bullets whistled around his ears and plunked into a ceiling support post and a corn bin flanking him.

The silhouetted figures screamed and danced, the wind whipping their hats from their heads and blowing their knotted bandannas around their faces like black guidons torn from burial shrouds. Flames from their guns angled toward the ground near their shuffling feet.

The bullets blew up sage branches and gravel.

Yakima's Colt thundered twice more, the blasts echoing around the stable and slamming against his ears like cupped hands, making his head swim.

A gun flashed a hundred feet ahead of him, from the murk at the rear corner of the unnamed saloon. Yakima winced as the bullet sliced a burning graze across the nub of his roughhewn, left cheek. He staggered backward, raised the Colt and triggered his left shot.

In the howling murk, a man groaned.

A shadow at the saloon's rear corner dropped.

Opening the pistol's loading gate, shaking out the spent shells and replacing them with fresh, Yakima walked toward the body forming a dark lump on the ground by the saloon. He replaced the spent cartridges with fresh from his belt, closed the loading gate, and spun the cylinder.

He looked around for more lurking shadows, saw none.

He squatted beside the dead man, turned him onto his belly.

Yakima scowled. "The marshal."

———

WHEN YAKIMA RETURNED to the saloon, the shadowy place was empty save for the bartender, Jake, standing behind the bar, leaning forward over an open newspaper.

The stove at the back of the place ticked. Leaping flames showed through a gap between its doors made by the bullet grooves in the left one.

A large beer and a steaming bowl sat on Yakima's table, near the stove.

The barman stared at him dully as he made his way to the room's rear. He was soaked from the rain that had washed the blood from his cheek. The fire felt good. He could hear the wind in the stove, wheezing like a baby dragon in a cage.

He returned the saddlebags to the chair, leaned his rifle against the chair, tossed his hat on the table, shrugged out of his deer hide coat, and slacked into his chair. He took a deep pull from the glass. The homemade ale and rotgut whiskey went down like a rare elixir. As he pulled the mug down from his mouth, he smiled.

He had his stake.

He'd soon visit Faith if only her crudely chiseled marker...and then he'd head down to Mexico and spend the winter with the senorita.

Faith wouldn't mind...

He'd just finished the rattlesnake stew, swabbing up the succulent remains with a chunk of crusty brown bread when Isabelle appeared, coming down the stairs angling out from the rear wall, ten feet beyond Yakima. The barman glanced at her without expression then turned back to his newspaper.

She walked down the steps, dragging the tips of her fingers along the knotted pole rail on her right. She looked at Yakima with those tan eyes between those waving tresses of Mexican-brown hair. She came over to his table, kicked out a chair, and turned to the barman, who was watching her now, expectantly.

She held up a single finger.

"Uno."

The barman turned around from his paper to fill a shot glass.

He brought it over and set it on the table then returned to his paper.

Yakima sat back in his chair, pulled his mug closer, and set his right ankle on his left knee.

She lifted the shot glass to her ripe lips, shaped a mysterious half-smile.

"Maybe now we will have some peace and quiet."

She'd heard the shots.

She took a small sip of the whiskey.

Yakima nodded. "Maybe." He frowned as he stared down at his beer. "The marshal…"

He looked up at her, curious.

She set her shot glass back down on the table, removed her hat, set it too on the table, and sat back in her chair. She crossed her long legs beneath her black wool skirt.

"Starrett's father," she said.

Yakima felt his lower jaw sag.

"They put on a show for you. Starrett takes care of the marshal in his old age," she said. "They are all"—she frowned, searching for the word—"*corrupto*." She made a slashing motion with her hand.

"Ahh." Again, Yakima frowned. "How did you know I…?"

"Had the money?"

"Yes."

"The old man knew the way old men know."

"Dark Moon."

She took another small sip of the whiskey, ran the pink tip of her tongue across her plump, upper lip, and smiled, tan eyes glinting shrewdly. "Besides, you were really coddling those saddlebags…like bambinos."

She smiled again. "They wanted to kill you because

they figured you were tracking them." She widened her eyes, sat back in her chair, and looked at him melodramatically from beneath her brows. "And I know who you are. Yakima Henry. Fierce fighter and man tracker. His home is his horse's back." Again, she smiled, her pretty cheeks dimpling, eyes flashing. "They say that."

Yakima sighed, cursed under his breath.

"My man is dead," she said. "Shot by Starrett."

"Why?"

Isabel shrugged a shoulder. "He wanted me."

"And he got you."

"Si."

Yakima scowled, disbelieving. "Why?"

"A man needs a woman. I needed a man." She sipped her whiskey. "I take care of my husband's father. I need money for that. It is the least I can do. My man, Red Elk, saved me from White soldiers, slave traders."

"You're alone."

She narrowed a shrewd eye at him. "As you are."

She picked up her glass again, between her thumb and index finger, and threw back the entire rest of the shot. She set the glass down on the table and rose.

"I sleep."

"Sweet dreams."

As she walked toward the stairs, she smiled over her shoulder at him as though she had a secret.

Yakima sat back and sipped his drink in the luxury of the comfortable chair and the warm, snapping fire. The barman said from behind the bar, "Take room four. Pay in the morning."

He turned a lamp low behind the bar then, yawning, went upstairs to bed.

Yakima remained in the chair, listening to the fire and the wind. When he finished his beer, he climbed the stairs. He didn't know how much time had passed when a soft tap sounded on his door.

"It's open," he said.

She came in, lit a lamp, and turned to him. She had a bottle in her hand. She set it on the table beside the bed.

"We are in town," she said, smiling. "We might as well live a little."

She wore only her shirt. She removed it, and the wavering lamplight caressed her bare skin, her high, proud breasts lovingly. She came to him, crawling beneath the covers. Tenderly, she kissed the graze on his cheek and snuggled up to him, ran her hand across his hard, broad chest, slid it down his flat, corded belly.

Yakima groaned.

———

HE WOKE WITH ANOTHER GROAN.

This was an agonized groan. A groan of pain.

He opened his eyes.

Crisp, golden, post-storm sunlight pushed through his dirty, flour sack-curtained window behind him and to his right. The light was like a dozen mini javelins piercing his eyes.

He looked to his left. The girl was gone. He looked at the chair.

He'd draped the loot-laden saddlebags over it.

They were gone.

He looked at the bottle on the table to his right.

Empty.

He grunted, winced painfully, touched his hand to his stitched temple. It wasn't the crease from the robbery that hurt. It was the hooch that hurt.

And whatever she'd laced it with. Some Indian concoction, most like.

He moved naked to the door, crossed the hall, and opened the door to the room she and Dark Moon had taken. Both beds were empty.

Gone.

He looked out the window between the empty beds.

It had to be mid-morning edging toward noon.

He cursed, turned in the empty doorway, and leaned against the frame, wincing as a mean little man savaged his brain with a hammer and a railroad spike in his head.

Gone.

He stared thoughtfully at the mud-brick wall on the other side of the hall.

He frowned, remembering.

Then he smiled.

"One shot."

His smile broadened.

The outlaws hadn't reacted though Indians weren't allowed hard whiskey in the unnamed saloon. They'd begrudged Yakima his. But they hadn't known he'd acquired the loot. Only the wise old Indian, Dark Moon, and the observant girl had known.

She hadn't been going to tell Starrett. She'd shuddered at his name.

Maybe she'd have some peace and quiet now.

Quite a gal.

"Oh, well," he said, resigned. He laughed. "Glad I could help, Isabel. Glad I could help."

Chuckling, he walked back down the hall toward his room, knowing he couldn't return to Pawnee. The law there would think he'd absconded with the bank loot. He'd mosey down to Arizona, to Mexico, without a stake.

A wanted man without a stake.

That was all right. He'd find something on the way. A man or men to kill...

And a grave to visit...

That was his life.

He winced again at the pain in his head. But it was hard to resent a beguiling waif such as Isabel, who'd done what she'd done so tenderly to fill his stormy night.

Faith wouldn't begrudge him.

A man needed a woman just as a woman needed a man.

"One shot!"

Laughing, he stepped into his room and closed the door.

END

*[Find Peter Brandvold's Yakima Henry novels
published by Wolfpack Publishing in various editions
including a boxed set of the entire series
on Amazon.]*

Wrong Side of a Bullet

A Short Story

By Nicholas Osborn

1

IT'S COMMON KNOWLEDGE THAT SAMUEL COLT GAVE US THE tool to tame the Wild West. We wielded gunpowder and lead with righteous fury, without a trace of remorse, and struck down every man who dared stand in the way of justice, until everyone knew the true law of the land—a bullet.

The revolver might've killed more men than we care to admit on its bloody mission, but even a fateful creation as fine as the six-shooter didn't have what it takes to kill the West. It was a steel behemoth—one that spewed flame and smoke, one that moved faster than anything seen before and roared its way into the future—that brought an end to the days of old. Dusty trails turned into two endless steel ribbons, a gallop on four hooves became a chugging of pistons and wheels, and a cowboy's call in the distance became a whistle of the inevitable. It was all coming to an end before it ever really got a chance to start. Some would call it a shame, others still would say it was for the best, but when the tracks were laid and the train came rolling into town, there wasn't anything that could be done about it. It just was.

The moral of the same story that birthed outlaws and gunslingers, saloon quick draws over a hand of poker and stagecoach robberies for a gold watch and ten dollars, even high noon shootouts erupting after a perfectly timed tumbleweed, is that time waits for no one. Progress took it all and replaced it with a revolution, leaving behind a lifestyle and culture, the beginnings of an idea about who we really were, to die in its wake. There's a funny thing about ideas, though. Sometimes they can be harder to kill than a pissed-off rattlesnake, and sometimes that rattlesnake could still get a lucky strike off every now and then.

Since 1869, we've learned the hard way that the Wild West wasn't just a time long gone or a fond memory of what once was. It was a stubborn, mean idea that would never back down and would never die. It doesn't take a cowboy hat and a pair of boots with a gun on your hip to see the world today is every bit as rowdy and unpredictable as it ever was. Some might even go as far as to say that the twenty-first century was a new kind of frontier, and there was no better place to see it in action than a bar just outside the county line, tucked away in the woods with a rather ironic name—*The Pine Box Bar.*

Ben Masterson had found himself in this very bar for the first time in his life, wondering how he'd never known about it before. For a man in his line of work, such a place could be exactly what he needed, when he needed it. All he had to do was show up and wait for everything to fall in place, just like it always had, collect a check and move on. If there were a hundred more just like it right down the road, he'd stop to have a drink in every single one of them, but he'd never been a man of luck his whole life. He was the kind of man who'd have to make do with what he had. Tonight, all he had was his last name and a note from a desperate woman in an all-too-familiar search for her man. That would have to be enough.

Against a constant humming of neon signs advertising beer, women, and women holding beer hung haphazardly on the wall and surrounded by a cloud of cigarette smoke, Ben propped himself on the end of the bar, doing his best to ignore several aging bullet holes that had gone unrepaired a few inches away from where he sat. It was a sign of good things to come as far as he was concerned. Drunken men, reckless firearms, and just enough money involved to get everyone all riled up was usually enough to convince him to stick around.

Ben lifted a single finger before his eyes followed suit, and he was met almost immediately with an impatient stare from a bearded, overweight bartender with more important things to do than wait on him to figure out what drink he wanted.

"Whiskey," said Ben. "Neat."

The bartender nodded and went to work, tossing a stained white towel over his shoulder as he flipped a glass tumbler between his fingers. He worked diligently and quietly, something Ben could easily find respect for.

———

DESPITE THE SWELL of laughs and curses from the men who filled the bar and the jukebox past its prime blaring a crying steel guitar, Ben was right at home because he had a pen in his hand and a blank piece of paper waiting.

The glass that slid his direction held an amber liquid that threatened to burn all the way down. It caught the flicker of neon, reflecting a blue and red glow that filled the room. He gently took half a swig and settled into the routine of sips that would carry him through the night.

Ben wore black leather boots with jeans to match, cuffed at the end, a starched white button-down covered with a thinly striped vest adorned with a golden pocket watch that had belonged to his family for generations. His cowboy hat had a traditional rancher crown but a brim that was twice as small as anyone else's. On his right pinky finger was a gold signet ring and in his left hand was a black pen without so much as a scratch on its surface. He sat the drink down and reached into a small leather bag he'd toted in and pulled out a stack of worn journals.

Ben looked like a man out of time, like he should've ridden up on a trusty old mare instead of his beat-up Ford pickup. He thumbed through the journal on top of the stack, scrolling over pages and pages filled from top to bottom with stories of his travels and work exploits. He was searching for where he left off last, but by the time he was flipping through the pages of the fourth journal in the stack, he started searching for any empty page he could find. The pages were records of stubborn men with stubborn ideas who refused to die, tales that would only be kept alive by the words he scratched down, and jobs that had kept him fed when he wasn't sure where his next meal would come from.

Finally, at the bottom of the pile, was a journal that didn't hold a single entry. When he'd found the blank page he'd been looking for, he tucked the rest of the journals away and prepared himself to continue his work. His pen hovered gently for a fleeting moment before the words came pouring out.

MY NAME IS BEN MASTERSON. *My great-great-grandfather was a lawman, a gambler, and a storyteller in his own right. He tamed Dodge City with a quick draw before doing the same to*

New York City with a stroke of his pen, but he couldn't dream of the things I've seen. Buried treasures that could be found only in the stars, legends that could kill, and divine tricks that could tear the world apart have all come at the hands of those with enough spine to pull the trigger. I may not be a lawman, but I'm as good as my ancestors at finding trouble and I know my way around at least one language well enough to pass it on. I'm no gambler either, so the gun that remains holstered at my side is used only to make sure the odds never go against me when I stand down the worst this world has to offer. I've traveled for years, finding lost husbands, tracking down family heirlooms, and gunning down any man who escaped the clutches of justice and there is one thing I can say without a shred of doubt. The Wild West is alive and kicking, like a mule with its nuts in a vice.

"YOU AIN'T TAKIN' a damn inch of what's mine, you hear me, you son of a—"

"It ain't *your* land, dumbass!"

Ben's eyes flicked up, only to catch a wiry man in a flannel shirt rolled up to his elbows, jabbing a finger toward a group of three other men gripping mugs of sloshing beer. With his finger curled at the end yet somehow still aimed right at those standing in front of him, the man's voice trembled with rage and his knuckles turned whiter by the second.

Ben watched the men bicker for a few seconds before he noticed the bartender's hand drift beneath the countertop and linger. Trouble was certainly coming, sure as the sunrise a few hours away, but it wasn't quite time yet.

His eyes fell back down to his journal, and his pen continued on.

• • •

THE WEST AIN'T JUST JINGLING spurs and sagebrush as far as the eye can see anymore. Its oil rigs pumping endlessly, truck stops bathed beneath sodium lights, small towns hugging outdated railways, and reservations where ancient songs still echo. Not everything is dead and gone, though. The same desperate determination that burned in the bellies of ranchers, lawmen, entrepreneurs, and families hard at work on their homestead was still burning as bright as ever in the hearts of men and women of the modern world. They want to build their own lives, make their own mistakes, forge their own future for the next generations, but everything goes against them. Things that cannot be understood work without end to bring ruin to their lives. I have seen as much.

"IF YOU DON'T WATCH your mouth, you'll be buried in that dirt you love so goddamn much. You hear me?"

"I would not hesitate to join those who came before me in death if it meant you would not step a single boot across my property line. I would rest peacefully in that dirt knowing my life had purpose." The wiry man was deadly serious when he spoke. "I would rather die than see it in the hands of men like you."

Ben once more pried his eyes from his writing. The argument was heating up, but it was still going in circles. There was a process to these types of things. Barroom scuffles were something of an art form all their own. If you are ever unlucky enough to find yourself in the middle of one more than a few times, the first thing you realize is everything is predictable. The shouting, the chest bumping, the insults, that split-second deep breath a man does before he hurls a haymaker, none of it comes as a surprise.

"There are things you don't know about, boy," one of the other men finally spoke up. He was calmer, but every bit as mean. "There are people you don't want to know, too. They ain't the kind to come bicker over a beer. They'll kill you before you ever see 'em comin'."

Ben couldn't help but scoff into his drink as he hid behind another casual sip of whiskey. The burn he first felt had given way to an earthy smoothness that coated his gums and tongue, and warmed his belly from deep down. After savoring one more sip, the pen seemed to hit the paper again with a life of its own.

I'VE BEEN CALLED a snake oil salesman, a grifter, cheat, killer, and worse. I'm not in this line of work for the fame, though. Since most of the people I work for are more broke than me, I learned a long time ago I better not be in it for the money, either. What keeps me going is the same thing that keeps me up at night. If all I leave behind are the tales of unspeakable things hidden in the shadows of our own lives, I'll know mine was a life well spent.

"I ALREADY GAVE Y'ALL A WARNIN', if I gotta do it again I'm kickin' every one of you out on your asses," threatened the bartender. "I ain't never seen a bunch of grown men bicker so much without havin' at least more than two drinks beforehand. You're all either gonna buy more booze or start swingin', because I ain't listenin' to your screamin' much longer."

The whole building fell silent after the tirade. Somehow, even the jukebox delayed rolling into its next song, like it knew better than to interrupt. That bartender knew his way around a threat, and he wasn't afraid to show it. Ben got the impression it wasn't his first time shouting down his own customers while also demanding they purchase more booze from his own establishment. If he had to take a guess, he'd probably say it accounted for around half of his business, and Ben was never one to judge how a man earned his living.

Regardless of whatever the bartender was trying to say, the men continued on doing exactly what they weren't supposed to do. Their shouts went back and forth, amplifying a little louder with each response. Ben knew what was coming next, he'd seen it time and time again already. So, he took another swig, sat the tumbler down gently on the countertop, and pushed his pen back to the journal.

HAVE YOU EVER SEEN COYOTE, the great Caddo trickster, stand as tall as a man and say things no man could say? I have. Did you know there exists in the world an ancient curse uttered first by Sitting Bull which could kill men right where they stand? I've held it in my hands. Have you felt the very foundations of the state of Texas tremble beneath the will of a single family betrayed by time? I've walked in their boots before. Beyond the cell phones and media and algorithms telling you what to think about the world just outside your door, there is something else entirely. We live in the remains of what has been, and no matter how deep I dig, there is always more to find. I've written tales truer than the oxygen I breathe now that would convince leaders around the world to build a grand asylum only to house myself. Tonight, sitting in a bar with a whiskey in one hand and a pen in the other, I think I might belong in that asylum.

BECAUSE THE TALE I'm about to tell is the most unbelievable of them all.

2

"DO YOU THINK WE WOULD NOT FIGHT BACK?"

"You don't wanna know what I think, asshole."

"Because we *will*. I might be standing alone in front of you, but when the fighting starts, and people start dyin', I won't be alone."

"I'm countin' on it."

"You'll wish you never said that."

The men couldn't get any closer. The outnumbered wiry one had puffed himself up and pushed against the chest of the closest bearded, overweight man with the swollen ego. Their faces were red and sweaty, their voices getting hoarse, and their fists were itching to get to work. The bar had devolved into a shouting match and the spectators were beginning to expect a show.

It was a fact of life that most were unwilling to admit to—people want to be in danger. There are families and hard workers and decent folk all around who don't know anything about such a lifestyle, but there are plenty of those who live in the underbellies of society, who are too afraid to leave the shadows cast down by a world that is leaving them behind. Those people live a different kind of life. It's the kind of life that will have you pounding cocktails at one in the morning in a bar notorious for gunfights, hoping that the people arguing in just a few feet away start throwing punches at each other.

The Pine Box Bar was packed full of those people, and they were doing exactly what they do best. They were cheering on a dangerous situation in the hopes it might turn deadly. They didn't care if they were caught in the crossfire, they weren't the kind of people who thought that far ahead. They just wanted to have a memorable night, and in their opinion, that wasn't too much to ask for.

Ben scribbled away, letting the chaos continue to unfold at no cost of his own. If anything, it helped him concentrate. A dull quietness never could bring words to mind quite like an argument could. He'd written some of his best drafts in the middle of a fight like this, and he didn't want to waste the opportunity. As much as he wanted to lose himself completely in the story that simply had to be told, he couldn't bring himself to do that just yet—because he was still living it.

WHEN THE TRANSCONTINENTAL *railroad had been completed by 1869, a new empire had been constructed right alongside it. It became the pulse of the United States of America, carrying goods and people from coast to coast, introducing a new way of life that few had even dared to dream of until then, and in doing so, revolutionizing the way we could see the world. The future would be forever changed because of what was accomplished. It would mean progress and prosperity for anyone lucky enough to be in the vicinity of that endless iron ribbon draped across the plains and over the top of mountains. It took an act of Congress and millions of dollars to build 2,000 miles of railway stretching from the Pacific to the Atlantic. It didn't just forever change travel and commerce though, it was said to have completely annihilated time and space, closing the furthest distances of a country eager to embrace their growing power.*

"Do you have a problem with money? Do you like bein' a broke, disgusting, piece of—"

"It could change your life," the next bearded man cut off his angrier, drunk friend. "More money than any of us would know what to do with."

"You'd be a damned fool not to take it and run." The angry one tried his best to sound cool and collected, coming across as twisted by his own rage instead.

"Then I will be a damned fool!" The wiry man had enough. He pushed past those standing in his way, shaking his head and whispering curses on his way to follow the advice of the bartender and get his hands on another drink.

The man who'd had enough plopped himself down on the bar just a few feet away from where Ben sat. He hollered for another drink that seemed to appear out of thin air right in his grasp, and was emptied only a second later. Another came without request this time, then another.

Ben left him alone. He tried to return to his writing, but he couldn't find the words just yet. He could feel the anger resonating from the man hell-bent on getting drunker by the second, and he knew there would be no words worth exchanging. His best bet would be to let whatever was about to happen play out.

"Red," came a sullen voice from none other than the bartender. "You been through all this before. Don't go to jail over it. Not again."

The wiry man still doing everything in his power to get as inebriated as possible made eye contact with the bartender. Tears began to well but his face couldn't get any redder than it already was.

"They won't take me to jail, they'll just kill me," said Red.

Red's words hung in the air like a storm cloud brewing just overhead. The Pine Box Bar wasn't just another hole in the wall serving piss-poor beer and over-priced Jim Beam. It was a crucible. Men like Red had forged their fates over a drink they shouldn't have had for longer than most realize. Ben had seen it firsthand plenty of times, men who were pushed to the edge, who were too caught up in their pride and ego to relinquish their grip on the one thing that will surely get them killed.

Finally, Ben went back to his work.

THE BUILDING of the railroad did more than lead to the rise of a new empire—it buried one too. The Lakota, the Cheyenne, the Apache, and countless other nations watched their world become sectioned and sold, severed by great iron tracks coursing throughout their homes like a cancer spreading without end. It's impossible to say how many Natives were displaced or killed at the hands of those same revolutionaries who would give us the railroad. Their homes were taken, their wild game slaughtered, their people deprived of everything they had known, and when they fought back, there was only more ruin waiting. Tens of thousands of foreign workers were imported to labor for such destruction. Some twenty thousand Chinese at one time toiled away on a fool's chance at a better life. Too many found themselves killed by nitroglycerin or worse, and those that survived were herded to any other industry that would have them. Chinese saw their deaths in the Sierra Nevada, the Irish on the plains, and Natives in their backyard. By the time the final spike had been driven, the government had paid millions to a few men who risked their lives to achieve something that had never been done before, at the expense of so many who had nothing to gain, who built the way to a future that never sought to include them. To some, the railroad was a testament to human potential, to others, it was a blade cutting through the heart of their home—and some of those scars have yet to heal.

ANOTHER DRINK SLID into Red's hand, its dull sound snapping Ben out of his own trance. He turned just in time to see Red chug the brown liquid as the same group of men approached him without a word. They did not aim to surprise, as Red stared them down the entire time he gulped his drink.

Ben took a sip of whiskey and twirled the pen in his fingers, anxious for what was to come. The air was tightening, like a storm just before the floodgates are opened and the thunder comes crashing down. People around the bar cleared a path first, then swarmed around to make sure they could get a clear view of what everyone was waiting on.

Red slammed his glass down, the sound sharp enough to turn every head that had been able to resist up to this point. "These people have been tryin' to take the ground beneath our feet since my ancestors taught them how to live. Why would they stop now? They know we will never stop fighting them."

"Don't do it, Red," the bartender threatened, ignoring everything Red was trying to tell him.

"I don't have a choice," Red admitted. "Neither do they."

This time, Ben finally had something to say. It was something that he couldn't ignore, even if it wasn't his time to intrude just yet. "Your ancestors," he began, speaking loud enough to draw the attention of both Red and the bartender. "Did they win many fights?"

"What is that supposed to mean?" The bartender couldn't help himself; he was lost.

Red wasn't, though. He knew exactly what Ben was talking about. "My ancestors beat the United States of America itself. We were the only ones to do so. A few drunks in a bar don't scare me none."

"I bet not," said Ben. "They say there wasn't anything that could scare Red Cloud's warriors. That is where you got the name, right?"

Red turned to stare Ben down. Shock washed over his face no matter how much he tried to hide it. The man's face was a map of defiance, his jaw set like stone.

Ben didn't respond to his endless glare, but he felt the pull of Red's words, like a current dragging him into the words he'd already written into his journal. He knew he'd already said too much, so he returned to his journal in the hopes that Red would not forget the reason he was at the Pine Box Bar tonight. Luckily, he had a group of men hell-bent on reminding him.

"You gonna run away from us every chance ya get?" A bearded man approached him, slapping him on the shoulder hard enough to let Red know it wasn't playful. "This ain't somethin' you can escape, it's comin' one way or another."

"He knows that." Another man flanked Red, also condescendingly patting him on the back. "He knows just how deep the shit he'd standin' in goes. We just gotta help him see it a little better, that's all."

Red turned to face his drunken assailants, balling up his fists as he did, knowing the time for words had most likely passed him by.

Ben should have listened to what he told the men, he should have paid attention to his surroundings a little better, because he was almost certainly at the center of the kind of fight that could turn deadly in a hurry. Instead, he pushed the pen to paper one more time and kept writing.

I'M HERE *tonight at the secret word of a woman worried about a man, the kind of story that has beget a million stories more throughout history. She knew he would be at the Pine Box Bar, she knew he would be doing something he shouldn't, but what she doesn't know is that they are the first to stand in the way of a new kind of revolution. Whispers of a new rail have started to pick up, and behind those whispers are the kind of financiers who could change the world with a stroke of their pen. I've followed those rumors here to Texas, and I expect to find out the truth about what is happening here one way or another. If there is one thing I've learned in my brief time as a detective-for-hire and freelancer, it's that the story no one can look away from always begins with one person's small problem spiraling out of control until it becomes everyone's problem. For people like those in the bar tonight, it's the kind of problem they've seen time and time again, for generations even, reborn yet again right under their noses. Unfortunately for them, I'm here to break the bad news to these modern-day pretend cowboys and outlaws, derelicts and degenerates, harlots, drunks, and every damned evildoer who'll listen...*

THE WEST MAY BE *alive again, but so is the dream that killed it.*

3

THE SOUND OF A MAN'S FIST CRACKING A MAN'S JAW IS ONE you can never get used to.

In a split second, the Pine Box Bar had turned from a powder keg to a full-blown explosion, with Red's fury sparking everything into motion. The first man he swung at went sprawling across a table that collapsed under his weight as soon as he collided with it. Wood splintered, glasses shattered, and the crowd that had gathered around roared to life like they'd been waiting all night to see blood. A neon Longhorn Brewery sign buzzed overhead, casting a deep red glow across the chaos unfolding.

Red didn't wait to see who would come at him next. With one man on his back, he turned to the next and prepared to do the same. A wild left hook came from nowhere, landing squarely on Red's jaw and sending a splatter of blood across the bar's countertop that was lost in the neon light. He didn't stop though.

His wiry frame became a blur as he ducked another wild swing, still coming to terms with the one that had rattled some teeth loose in his head, then answered his own wildly thrown strike to a man's gut on his right.

Four against one, and the vultures were circling.

Each punch struck like a hammer on iron, echoing through the bar, broken only by the swells of cheers and groans of the recoiling from the brutality unfolding. The bar became a pit in a matter of seconds, with tables and chairs and bottles and mugs being used for weapons alongside fists and teeth and anything else the men could hurl without mercy. Fights like these were once the pulse of the Wild West. Beneath the humming neon and surrounded by cell phones aimed at the fight like firearms, it was as if the past and future collided violently.

The bartender's screams were drowned out with ease. He tossed his apron aside, opting to leave the sawed-off shotgun still hanging beneath the countertop in Ben's sight. He did his best to break the fight up, but it seemed nothing could stop the inevitable, and the bartender wound up being a participant in the fight himself more than a catalyst to bring it to an end.

Ben, meanwhile, did his best not to spill his drink over the journal he was writing in, and decided he could jot down a few more words while he still could.

A NEW IRON horse is threatening to return to the lands of those who couldn't stop its predecessor. A new train is coming, one built in the Lone Star State with a name that felt right at home—a bullet. Fifty miles an hour was once a radical speed to travel on rails stretching from coast to coast, but the world has long since changed. Two hundred miles an hour can be seen as frightfully slow compared to what technology has given us today, but the rumors I've heard do not tell a story of how we can catch up to the rest of the world, they tell the story of a new revolution, a technological advancement believed to be impossible to achieve.

They'll call it progress, but we already know what that means.

"I'LL KILL you for that, you son of a—"

The shattering of glass broke up one drunken man's threats, sending shards flying in Ben's direction. He swept off the smallest pieces of glass from his journal, reached for his tumbler that was almost empty, and took another sip. His eyes scanned the room until he saw Red in the back corner, swinging with relentless fury, and that's when he noticed the fight was no longer just fists. It looked like the butt of a rifle flying through the air, gripped in both of Red's bloody hands, it twirled and spun and struck with a blunt force that could be felt across the room.

To Ben's surprise, Red had brought a gunstock war club to the fight, and he looked damned determined to show the men standing against him exactly what it could do. There might have been more suspicions lingering in Ben's head than he cared to admit, but when he saw the weapon being used, there was one thing that immediately became clearer than ever. Red came to the bar ready to go to war.

It moved like it had a will of its own, even though Red was holding it, the war club was guided by something else entirely. It left behind carnage on its victims that seemed to defy the laws of flesh and bone. One man caught a blow to the shoulder and crumpled to the floor with his arm hanging uselessly at his side. He groaned and rolled and clawed to get away, but Red brought down another merciless strike to the back of his head, and the man fell silent right where he lay.

Ben watched as Red wielded the gunstock war club with ease, splattering blood and splitting flesh at will against the men who started something they weren't prepared to finish. One man managed to swing the back-side of a chair at Red, but the club met it midair, shattering the wood into splinters cast out in every direction.

As the fight raged on, Ben put pen to paper to take advantage of the last few moments he had left.

REVOLUTIONS RARELY BEGIN how you would expect. They are not met with grandeur or applause, they are not brought into the world on a red carpet or revealed behind a closed curtain. They barrel into the world, causing devastation for anything in its relentless wake. This new kind of bullet is said to once again carve through sacred land, a new scar on ground already bleeding. It may bring forth a new era of prosperity, but it will not be for everyone. Not for the ones who've held this earth in their own hands since the stars were young, not the ones who still hear the whispers of their kin in the wind.

A SKULL CRACKING sent screams throughout the bar, interrupting Ben's writing once more with the garish sounds of unadulterated violence. There were two men down on the floorboards struggling to stand again, and two men still coming at Red with one thing on their mind. Red swung that club like it was the last thing he'd ever do in his life. It was the kind of weapon that didn't just hit men, it haunted them. Neon glow painted Red's face in shades of blood and shadow, his eyes burning with rage, not of his own, but of something long forgotten. It was as if his own ancestors had taken up arms against the men who were threatening him. He swung and swung and swung, lost in the hate and adrenaline pumping through his veins.

Two of the bearded drunkards still circled Red as the

war club continued to sing its deadly song, whistling through the air with unmatched precision. He didn't notice the other men who had abruptly chosen sides in the middle of the fight, their bravado chipped away by the bodies groaning at Red's feet, but not quite broken just yet. One clutched a broken bottle, its jagged edge glinting with lethal intent. The other, a burly man with a face only his own mother could love, brandished a folding pocketknife that flickered in and out of sight.

"We're all gonna die here tonight!" Red shouted while adjusting his grip on the war club. "You might kill me, but they'll find your bodies too, lying in a puddle of *my* blood."

"Don't matter," one man growled. "You'll be dead."

The fight continued. The man with the bottle lunged, aiming for Red's ribs, but Red sidestepped, the club high above his head, coming down with a crack that sent the bottle—and the hand holding it—sprawling across the floor. The man howled, clutching his shattered wrist, and staggered back into the crowd, desperate to hide his face. His partner with the pocketknife hesitated, his blade trembling slightly, but his eyes still held onto a desperate glint. He wasn't backing down, not yet.

Ben couldn't help but watch the bar descend into hell. Despite the chaos, he gripped the pen a little tighter and kept scribbling. He wrote fast, the words spilling out like they were trying to keep pace with the war club humming through the air.

FOR GOOD OR BAD, *what I am chasing is bound to change the future around the world, but for now, it comes down to a phone call about a woman who has lost a man, a woman who is deathly afraid of what may happen. It's benign, sure, but it's also just the beginning. She didn't give me a name, or at least not one that could be spoken by men today. She told me where I should go, trembling and terrified and looking over her shoulder the whole time, and she told me what I might find. I didn't believe her at first, even if I knew I had no choice but to go, but I understand now.*

RED WAS BACKED INTO A CORNER, his heavy panting masked by the crowd's cheers. He was fending off a pocketknife with a weapon three times as large, and he knew he held the advantage. The man standing in front of him made his move. He slashed quick, aiming for Red's throat. He might've missed his jugular, but he tore through fabric and sliced through Red's shoulder, forcing him to howl in pain as he tried to get out of the knife's way. Before the man wielding the knife could take advantage of the lucky strike, Red brought the gunstock war club up from his side, swinging underhanded with every bit of strength he could muster, catching his opponent right under the chin with a sickening crunch. The blade rattled to the floor first, followed by a heavy thud of the now-unconscious knifeman. His eyes rolled into the back of his head for a split second before he fell silent.

Red looked around as the shushing fell over the bar. He thought he'd finished the fight on his feet. He even allowed a smirk to begin to curl on his lips as his club dripped with blood at his side. Standing alone, surrounded by drunks and overly-eager designated drivers who'd gotten more than they bargained for, Red looked like a man satisfied with the day's work he'd just put in.

Ben was still writing frantically, trying to get his final words in before the inevitable end of such a fight. Carnage like this might start with fists and blunt weapons, but the fury of hellfire itself is always waiting.

. . .

THE MAN I came here to see is here, and his name is written in blood on a club made for war.

AN ALL-TOO-FAMILIAR CLICK turned the already distraught bar upside down, finally breaking Ben's concentration for good, and setting into motion his whole reason for showing up. It was almost like he yanked the gun from the holster himself by what he wrote, but if he was going to do anything about the end of the barrel suddenly pointed at Red's back, he'd knew have to use something a heck of a lot mightier than a ballpoint pen.

4

NEVER TRUST A MAN SITTING ALONE IN A BAR.

He might be too drunk to notice what's going on around him, or there might be something worse going on inside his head than drowning out his own thoughts. A safe general rule of thumb is to assume anyone you don't know probably has a gun tucked in their pocket, and they are more than likely willing to use it under the right circumstances. If you see them drinking, you better just assume they are feeling a little more apt to using said gun.

There wasn't a single soul still breathing at the Pine Box Bar that assumed Ben was anything other than some mindless drunk scribbling away in a journal. They never really paid him enough attention to see anything different, but that wasn't Ben's fault.

Red was standing with his back against a wall, his chest heaving, the gunstock war club slick with blood in his grip, his eyes darting back and forth, waiting for whoever had the stomach to step up next. The bar had become a blood-soaked graveyard of splintered wood and shattered glass. Neon signs buzzed as if nothing had ever happened, their red and blue and yellow glow emanating in every direction. Despite the crowd of people that had just witnessed the devastation unfold, the bar was eerily quiet.

A sudden shout cut through the silence. "You think you're untouchable, Red?" The voice came from the burly man with the weathered face, now back on his feet, blood trickling from his brow. He'd found a pocketknife on the floor that didn't belong to him, but between the three-inch blade in one hand and the three-inch snub-nose revolver in the other, he was feeling more confident by the second.

Behind him, two more men staggered up to their feet, one nursing a broken wrist, doing his best to hide the waves of pain that were washing over him, and the other pulling out a rusty, old revolver.

Cell phones were still shining down on the fight, but the faces holding them were no longer present. The drunks had managed to find cover behind everything from a bench seat booth to a bar table, videoing everything except their own irresponsibility.

In the commotion of a bar fight getting ready to turn into a gunfight, there wasn't anyone with enough wits to watch the lone man drinking at the bar, scribbling nonsense away, keeping to himself. There were few instances of luck showing its face in Ben's line of work, but even he could appreciate even a passing glance every now and then. He slid his journal into his bag, making sure that his movements were slow and deliberate. His fingers brushed the cold steel of a S&W revolver that had earned its way into the world record books. The custom 327 model was a perfect combination of old West grit and modern sensibility, chambered in 9mm with an eight-round cylinder, it always gave him a couple of extra surprises to the criminal connoisseur who thought counting to six was the way to stay alive. He'd finally put down the Colt his grandfather gave him, stripped the 327 down to its iron sights and tucked it away in an old leather holster fifteen years ago, and it hadn't left his side since. On nights like this, it was all the safeguarding he needed.

He'd come to the Pine Box Bar to begin a story, not to end one, but the air was thick with the promise of more death to come. Red's war club, as strangely in tune with life and death as it was, wouldn't outrun bullets. Those men knew it just as well as Ben. What they didn't know was why Ben cared enough to stand up from his seat when the fight looked like it was finally coming to an end.

"Stay out of this," Red growled in Ben's direction, his voice low. He twirled the war club, its carved wood catching the neon light, but his eyes never left the men closing in.

"I'll shoot every son of a bitch here if you take one more step," the bearded man threatened, still keeping his gun aimed at Red's back. "Startin' with this one."

Ben didn't answer. He pulled the revolver free of its home in the leather holster, the weight familiar in his hand, spurring a thousand memories of every time he squeezed the trigger. It was cocked and aimed before anyone could blink. The man who promised Red's death just a moment ago was now contemplating his own life.

The crowd gasped as the bartender was the first to see the inevitable and ducked behind the counter, still holding the shotgun he'd likely never fire. The bar was a keg of gunpowder about to blow, it just needed a spark.

Bam.

The bearded man made up his mind, choosing to unleash the hounds of hell right into Red's back. He tried to recover in a hurry, swinging his arm to where Ben stood, but he couldn't take back what he'd already set in motion.

Ben squeezed gently, allowing the recoil of the revolver to concentrate in his dominant hand, tracing its way up through his arm and into his shoulder, his tight grip forcing the end of the barrel to stay just where it had been a fraction of a second before the bullet blasted out. He moved with ease, squeezed the trigger again and again, then dropped below the counter before anyone could muster the strength to sling lead back his direction.

The gunshots cracked like thunder through the tin-covered bar out in the piney woods. Every person still sucking air inside scattered like cockroaches beneath a boot. Red collapsed to the ground, crawling with one arm beneath the nearest table, clutching his side in pain. One burly man collapsed right next to him, but didn't move. Three men answered the call, flashing their own firearms before bailing from the fight behind the nearest wall.

Tucked behind the sturdy bar, Ben felt comfortable in the cover he'd given himself. Bullets slammed inches away from where he sat, sending wood splintering in every direction after a dreadful *thump, thump, thump* of the lead sinking into lumber. A brief pause was all he was looking for, and when it came, he didn't waste any time.

Ben swung wide with both arms outstretched, gripping the revolver with surreal precision, he squeezed the trigger and one man fell back grabbing frantically at his chest.

Just as he went to change targets, another popped his head up from behind the pool table, taking just one second too long to find where Ben was shooting from. Ben sent a 9mm bullet right through his forehead, letting him fall on his back dead, staring endlessly at the tin ceiling donning a few more holes than it had the night before.

Ben leaped back behind cover, allowing his opponents to unload their magazines into the wall behind him or the bar that had already saved his life half a dozen times over. After another lull in the firing, Ben went back to work.

This time, they were waiting on him.

He popped his head out just in time to hear a bullet whistle by, grazing his cheek and sending a stream of blood pouring down the side of his face. He yelped and threw himself back behind the bar where he'd come.

The man who'd taken the lucky shot cursed, firing wild as he watched his target flee, the bullets shattering a bottle on the shelf behind Ben. Liquor rained down, stinging Ben's eyes as he rolled to the side, glass crunching under his boots as he crawled for safety. Any advantage he'd had before the fight started was long gone now.

With Red still bleeding out beneath a table to his right, Ben was the only target left for the few men with fight still in them, and they were all too eager to bet their lives on those odds. The poor man who went first had no chance. The first step he took to flank Ben around the corner of the bar would be his last he'd ever take on this earth. As soon as his boot hit the floor in front of where Red was lying, the sharp end of the gunstock war club came down with a spurt of blood, piercing right through the top of his foot until it sank into the wooden floorboards. The man screamed, fell to the floor grasping at his wound and crying out. He never saw the second swing aimed at his temple. The sound of Red's war club colliding with his skull was louder than any gunshot. The man fell silent just as his partner turned to run the other direction.

Red's adrenaline-fueled scream filled the air as the final drunk acted on the realization that he was in over his head. "Get him!" he roared to Ben.

Ben scrambled to his feet, heart pounding, the bar a blur of motion and noise and violent catastrophe. The crowd was screaming now, seemingly spurred on by Red's haunting howls. Some were still scattering, diving for cover, others bolted for the door, hoping to escape with their lives. Cell phones fell, screens cracking on the floorboards. The Longhorn sign flickered, casting wild shadows as Ben gently allowed his aim to fixate on the man fleeing the bar.

Just when the man thought he'd find cover in the crowd trying to fit through the front door all at once, Ben squeezed the trigger. The people trying to leave had no choice but to assume the worst. A complete stranger had just opened fire into a swarm of innocents. Despite their fear, their screeches of terror, and their understandable desperation, it was only the coward who fell to the floor when it was all said and done. He hit the floorboards with a thud, his rusty revolver skittering into the chaos of fleeing feet. Blood pooled beneath him, seeping into the cracks of the Pine Box Bar's worn wood.

Ben's ears rang, the S&W 327 still warm in his grip, its eight-round cylinder down to its last two surprises. He crouched behind the bar, his cheek stinging where the bullet had grazed him, blood mixing with the liquor dripping from his hair. Gunpowder and fear lingered in the air, the kind of stench that clung to your skin and never let go.

Red's roar echoed again, raw and primal, pulling Ben's eyes to the corner where he was bleeding on the floor. His war club still gripped in his bloodied fist. He was trying to drag himself up, one hand clutching his bleeding side, the other dragging the club with a fury that seemed to defy the bullet that had just torn through his flesh seconds ago.

Gunshots and screams turned to guttural groans of those left bleeding in the floor and heavy panting from those able to breathe. Neon hummed like nothing ever happened, the pool table now stained in splatters of blood sat vacant. There wasn't a single glass still sitting on the bar that hadn't been blown to pieces by gunfire. Cell phones lay cracked and forgotten, their lights shining into the air like a movie set gone horribly wrong.

Ben's heart pounded as he glanced at Red, their eyes meeting for a split second—a nod, a pact sealed through bloodshed.

A low, hollow scrape broke the silence, not from the bodies strewn across the floor, but from behind the bar. The bartender, who'd retreated to safety behind the cover of his bar rose slowly, his sawed-off shotgun gripped tight in trembling hands. His face, pale and sweat-slick, twisted into something new—greed, maybe, or desperation. He stepped out from the counter, the barrel of his gun trained on Red.

"Thought you could just walk in here and tear my place apart? How many times have I told you this is what happens to men like you? How many times did I tell you that you'd get killed comin' here?" The bartender spat after he spoke, his voice was sharp with a confidence he hadn't shown before. "It looks like you gonna have to learn the hard way. Some people can't learn."

He lifted the shotgun slowly, aiming at Red with both barrels.

Ben followed suit, popping up from behind the bar with his trusty revolver aimed at the bartender's chest. A smirk formed on his lips just as the bartender shot his eyes in his direction.

"I been watchin' you, stranger, countin' every shot.

You ain't got nothin' in that fancy gun of yours. I don't know who you are, but I gotta assume you're here for the price on this bastard's head just like the rest of those pricks who shot up my place of business. I got news for you, that money is as good as mine now."

"You go ahead and do whatever you think you need to do."

"Cocky little shit, ain't you?" The bartender finally swung his shotgun over to Ben. "Red's corpse oughta pay to rebuild this bar and then some. It's only fair."

Ben's grip tightened on the S&W still in his fist. The bartender's count was off. Six was

the way things used to be, he just needed to wait for the right time to strike, just like before. He stood slowly, keeping the revolver low, his face a mask of calm despite the blood dripping down his jaw. "You sure about that?" he said, voice steady, cutting through the neon hum.

The bartender's confidence faltered, but he held his ground, the shotgun's twin barrels gleaming. "Don't play games. I know you're bluffin'." He shifted his aim toward Red once again.

Ben didn't hesitate. He drifted his aim slightly to the left and squeezed the trigger, the 9mm bullet screaming past the bartender's head, shattering a bottle on the shelf behind him. Glass exploded, liquor sprayed into the air like rain, and the crack of the shot echoed again through the tin-roofed bar. The bartender flinched, his shotgun wavering, but his eyes lit up with a reckless glint. "I might've miscounted, but you missed your last shot," he sneered, leaning his head down to aim the shotgun at Red. "Time to cash in."

Red growled from the other side of the bar. Somehow, he found the strength to raise his war club, even though the bullet in his side slowed him.

The bartender's finger tightened on the trigger. "Say goodbye, you—"

Ben squeezed the trigger. The final 9mm round in the cylinder exploded out, ripping through the air until it punched through the bartender's chest before he could fire. The shotgun clattered to the floor as the man staggered, eyes wide with shock, blood blooming across his shirt. He collapsed, a wet gurgle escaping his throat, his body joining the others in the bar's blood-soaked grave.

The neon still buzzed, unbroken, casting its ominous red glow throughout what was left of the bar. Ben lowered his revolver, its cylinder spent, but the weight heavier than ever. Red slumped back against the table, his war club falling to his side, his breath shallow but steady. Their eyes met again, but no words came out.

The Pine Box Bar had earned its name yet again, and the night wasn't even done with them yet.

5

"How'd you know I'd be here?"

"Let's just say you have a secret admirer."

"She finally made the call."

"Seems so," said Ben. "Said she was worried about you, that you were gettin' in too deep, pissin' off a bunch of people more dangerous than you realized. She's scared."

"Kaya, she tends to worry too much," admitted Red. "She's got a good heart, though."

"From the looks of it, she should've been more worried for these guys."

A bizarrely needed, but wholly unwelcome laugh burst out between them. Standing in the middle of the remains of what was left of the bar, amid pools of blood, shattered glass, the stench of death, and the haunting gunpowder-laced scent that hovers in the air after a fire-fight—Ben and Red were the only ones left standing. There had to be some joy in that simple fact.

They weren't the only ones breathing, though. A few dying gasps exhaled by one man lying in the middle of them faded into nothingness, but there was one more still holding on, trying to escape the inevitable.

The burly man with the weathered face—the one who'd sparked this hell—was somehow still alive, slumped against a wall surrounded by bullet holes. For reasons no one there could explain, they all missed, creating a nearly perfect silhouette of holes and splintered wood where he sat. Blood bubbled on his lips, his hand reached over and over again in a vain search for his snub-nosed revolver that was already long gone. His eyes glazed over, but he was still locked onto Red, unearned self-righteousness burning like coal in his sunken stare.

"A revolution is coming," he forced the words out between fluid-filled coughs, each one a labor that might end his life right then and there. "You can't stop it. No one can."

Red's war club twitched, sending a few drops of blood to hit the floor, but not before it swelled with a strange sensation between his grip. For a fleeting moment, it looked like it was absorbing the blood, even relishing it, like its thirst had been quenched or its hunger quelled. It was drenched in red one moment, yet polished and perfected the next.

Ben couldn't help but stare at the weapon Red had toted into the bar and was now propped up on, leaning like he'd give way without its support. He watched the gunstock war club soak in the violence, the mayhem, the waves of blood crashing against its surface only to become lost in the heat of battle. There was something unspoken about the club, something ancient that could not be described. Luckily, for the moment, Ben only had to appreciate the fact that it wasn't being swung at his head.

He finally turned his attention to the dying man, his own S&W dangling uselessly at his side. "You ain't gonna live to see mornin', so that don't matter much for you now, does it?"

The man's laugh was a gurgle. His head lolled, eyes dimming, before a final threat escaped his lips. "A bullet is coming for you too, boy. All of you. From sea to shinin' sea."

Ben stood, meeting Red's gaze at last. The warrior's face was stone, but his wounds spoke of a fight far from over. "We've stopped men like him before," Red said, voice rough as gravel. "But we can't stop what's comin'. We could kill a thousand men who think and look just like him, but two thousand more will replace them, and they will all come for what is mine."

"Can't stop the future from happening," said Ben, making sure he holstered his revolver and retrieved his backpack carrying all of his journals. "Can only make room for it," he said with a knowing glance in Red's direction.

"We may have won this fight, but a war is brewing and the lines have already been drawn. It is our right to hold them until our dying breath. The men you are chasing don't care about those lines or anything that might stand in the way of those rails. Men like that only care about one thing."

"What's that?"

"Their revolution," said Red.

They listened to the endless hum of the neon as the last remnants of gunpowder in the air drifted away into nothing. They stood still, each coming from different worlds, carrying their own pasts and regrets and dreams.

"What are you gonna do now?" Ben broke the silence.

"I could ask you the same."

"You could."

Red allowed the war club to *thunk* softly to the floor, still tight in grip as he made his way to the door, dragging over bodies, debris, and beer. He turned to look at Ben one more time before he spoke with a look in his eye which betrayed the question that came from his lips.

"Whose story are you gonna tell, Mr. Masterson?"

Ben's journal called to him from inside his bag, its pages demanding a tale of blood, bullets, and a man fighting a revolution with his bare hands. The first railroad birthed a new era of mankind, tearing through lands and lives with iron and steam, thrusting the world into an industrial age whether they wanted it or not. This new bullet train born in Texas was its heir, hungry for sacred earth, backed by men who'd kill to pave its path and in doing so, etch their own name into the pages of history.

Some revolutions rolled on, chugging along without end as if they were guided by the hands of fate and progress, but Ben saw the fire in Red's eyes, and he felt that same burning deep down in his own gut.

A new kind of bullet was coming for them, one that could only be stopped dead in its tracks by gunpowder and lead.

Woman With No Eyes

A Short Story

By Kathleen O'Neal Gear

Woman With No Eyes

THE AIR IS SO cold it has a strange unearthly presence.

Frozen fog eddies over the low hills, seemingly alive. In the movements, I see shapes appear and disappear.

I lift a gloved hand to shield my eyes from the brilliant glare. My horse's hooves slip on ice. People laugh nervously as they gaze out across the vast frozen plains. A soldier in blue lifts a canteen, another soldier spurs his horse into a trot. I am the only woman here. The only living woman. I'm holding tight to my reins. One of the journalists calls out to another, a tall man with a cadaverous face in a heavy wool coat. They ride close, exchange words. The Indians, Sioux, would have walked here, measuring distance not in days but in sleeps.

"Is this it?" I ask. "Is this the battlefield?"

As usual, the Sioux policeman who is my escort does not answer.

"How will I know when we reach the battlefield?" I say.

Red Hawk blinks, bows his head briefly.

He rarely answers my questions, but murmurs, "She has no eyes."

"What?"

He says something under his breath. I assume he's speaking Sioux, maybe swearing. His words hang in the air like smoke signals. He rides away from me without explanation. General Miles told me to stick close to Red Hawk, for he is one of the few Sioux that speaks English, which he learned at the Indian school.

I kick Windrunner, my horse, and follow Red Hawk down the hill into an open area surrounded by deeply eroded cliffs that resemble ancient faces staring down upon us.

Red Hawk veers around something on the snowy ground.

I do the same, but abruptly pull back on the reins. Windrunner dances sideways as though to avoid it. The little girl, a toddler, rests on her back, staring sightlessly at the sky. I see no bullet wounds. The toddler's frozen eyes are gray and open wide, staring sightlessly at the sky. A woman lies face down a short distance away. A scrap of faded red blanket covers her hair and is tied beneath her chin. Her outstretched arms resemble twisted rags. She must have reached for her crying baby until the very end. I pass two more children.

The humps covered with snow. Red Hawk was right. My eyes did not see.

A breeze trails more snow across the corpses, wafting the scent of death...but the smell is cloying, gagging. Sickness rolls through me.

I know the story. On December 28th of last year, the 7th Cavalry reached the Sioux camp near Wounded Knee Creek. The Sioux leader, Big Foot, saw them coming, raised a white flag, and informed the soldiers that his people would surrender peacefully. On the 29th, Colonel James Forsyth herded them into this clearing, had the Sioux men form a council circle, and surrounded the circle with his cavalry. He positioned four Hotchkiss mountain guns, revolving cannons firing 1.65-inch explosive shells, on a hilltop above the clearing.

I scan the hills, wondering which one. *Ah, that one. There is a swath of fresh earth that is not covered with snow. The mass grave that was dug about two weeks ago?* The soil must be warmed by the decomposing bodies.

When Forsyth ordered that all weapons be confiscated, the Sioux donned their sacred ghost shirts and began to dance. Many of the Sioux had already given up their weapons. When the 7th Cavalry opened fire, they were defenseless. Around three hundred died. Twenty-five soldiers were killed.

Windrunner stamps his feet as though he, too, is freezing and wants to run away from this place.

What am I doing here?

Three weeks ago, I had an entertaining bylined column on the editorial page of the *Chicago Herald* called "Snap Shots." In my free time, I labored over my new book on beauty advice. All of that faded on December 29, 1890, when the Wounded Knee fight vaulted into the headlines. Absently, I read the news about the Ghost Dance, which seemed a very tame affair, no more threatening than the revivals in Chicago. I had no idea why Indians leaping around, worshipping their messiah with chants and prayers, scared anyone. They were just praying for the return of the buffalo, for their ancestors to rise from their graves, and for Whites to vanish from the earth. Fantasy, of course. Why should anyone care? Then my editor, Jimmy Scot, called me into his office and asked me if I was brave enough to head to the center of the conflict at Pine Ridge and "tell what you think about the Indians."

"I've only been a reporter for fifteen months. Why me?"

"Just talk to people. Try to find the truth."

I boarded the train on January 12th, 1891.

Desolate country passed by through the window. Occasionally, there were deer or antelope, but mostly there no wild animals, just cattle, horses, pigs. A few dogs trotted along the tracks with their ribs sticking out like iron bars. We passed towns. Wagons. People.

When the train clanked into Rushville, Nebraska, I gathered my things and worked my way to the door along with the other passengers. Everyone was polite. There's no shoving or rancor, which is so common in Chicago. The first thing I noticed as I stepped down to the platform was the armed men in blue. Soldiers packed the dirt streets. Spurs jingled. Swords flashed. Horses and wagons rattled by.

The next morning I joined a mule-driven Army transport headed to Pine Ridge. We passed over a thousand teepees. Picturesque, bathed in woodsmoke. Nearby, dozens of white military tents stood. Soldiers seemed to be everywhere.

My ugly little driver kept me entertained.

"Don't you worry none, Miz Dean, we'll be at the Chicago Herald shack in no time."

We passed a few Indians draped in filthy blankets. Their face paint was fabulous. I'd have to think about how to use that in my book on beauty advice. "Are they Sioux?"

"Yes, ma'am, and they are plaguers. Don't get too close to 'em."

"Plaguers?"

"Yes, ma'am, suffering from whooping cough,

measles, tuberculosis and influenza, and probably a hundred other things."

"Their faces are gaunt, Mr. Sanders. They appear to be starving."

"Well, I don't know about that, but they complain all the time that the Pine Ridge agent claims he gives them a month's worth of food and it only lasts two weeks."

"Do you think they are simply wasteful?" I asked.

"Oh, yes, ma'am. No doubt about that."

He slapped the reins and the mules picked up the pace. The wagon rocked and squealed.

"Back in town, except for soldiers, I saw very few White men and women on the streets. Where are the townspeople?"

"Behind locked doors, ma'am. Didn't you see that war paint they're wearing? The Indians are mad as all get out. No telling what they'll do next." He gave me an askance look. "Begging your pardon, but I can't for the life of me understand why your newspaper would send a woman out here. It's way too dangerous."

"Is it?"

He gave me an astonished look. "Pretty, stylishly dressed, blonde lady like you? You better hope the savages don't get their hands on you."

I pulled my notebook and pencil from my coat pocket. "I would be very interested to hear your opinion of the Indian situation, sir."

"Well, it's dire, ma'am. Don't matter that they been confined to reservations, they're still out and about, thieving, knocking on doors, pleading for food. They are beggars most supreme. And they're always filthy. I swear a rattlesnake won't even bite 'em for fear of contamination."

I jotted down notes. "Do you know that Eastern newspapers describe the Indians as noble and abused?"

"Well, they ain't never been here, have they? Elsewise, they'd know none of that's true. They're devils, pure and simple. Ain't no place in the world for them, if you ask me, and that's the truth."

The wagon bumped over a boulder, forcing me to grab hold of the seat. When we passed close to a teepee, I saw an infant in a cradleboard leaned against a rock. The baby bawled loudly.

I frowned in wonder. "Mr. Sanders, I have been told that Indian babies never cry. But that one is crying just like a white child. I am surprised. The babies at least have generous streaks of human nature."

"Oh, you may think so, but a few years from now that little fella will take his war axe and hack you to pieces without a second thought."

Sanders drove toward a collection of ramshackle buildings and military tents. He stopped in front of a wooden structure that looked like it might collapse at any instant. "This is it, ma'am. This is the Chicago Herald shack."

I nodded. "It certainly is a shack."

Sanders trotted around to help me down, then tipped his hat to me. "Pardon me, ma'am, but I have to be off. Have to report to the commander. Good day to you."

"Thank you, sir."

When I shoved open the door, every person in the smoke-filled room turned and went silent. Journalists had arrived from across the country, all men, of course. I could tell from their scowls that they, like Mr. Sanders, did not approve of my being here. After a brief interval, they returned to their loud conversations.

Over the noise, an unknown man yelled, "It's Teresa Dean, isn't it? I'm not about to share the newspaper's shack with a woman! You'd better turn around and head straight back to Chicago before you lose those pretty blonde curls."

"Afraid of the competition, sir?" I shouted.

He threw his head back and laughed.

The fools. They were partly responsible. Correspondents had hurried west in the fall of last year intent upon reporting on the war. Instead, day after day, the reservation remained quiet and calm, so they took it upon themselves to invent stories. They made up rumors, stoked gossip, and wrote out-and-out lies of rampaging Indians intent upon slaughter, all the while scrawling chapters for lurid dime novels. People in Chicago found it thrilling. People in the West found it terrifying.

My first dispatch to my editor on January 16th noted: "The only people at the reservation who seemed to be at all conscious of danger" were the reporters. I openly charged that they were reckless and hateful. They invented sensational threats that did not exist. It was rampant fearmongering.

Jimmy Scot refused to publish it.

A few days later, I walked up to a knot of reporters who were staging a photo. They had borrowed carbines, cartridge belts, knives and revolvers, and arranged them in front of Indian lodges to create a threatening scene. John B. McDonough of *The World* was setting up the camera.

"What are you doing?" I asked.

McDonough waved a hand at me. "Get back! I've been telling the people back home what a dangerous assignment this is. If I send back a picture with a woman correspondent in it, I'll be the laughingstock of my New York friends."

"Really? My presence might make your readers suspect that you are lying about the impending massacres and bloody battles you've been writing about? You are a liar, sir."

The other reporters gathered around me and physically forced me out of the picture.

I visited the agency's chapel, where Indian women and children, wounded in the battle, lay sprawled across the floor. The screams of pain were horrific. With one exception. There was a little boy with half his jaw and throat shot off. He made no sound, just stared up at me with huge black eyes. That horror will never leave me.

...Windrunner snorts and leaps ahead, drawing me back to this vast desolate battlefield. "Whoa! Whoa, boy. Everything's all right."

The horse settles down to a skittish prancing, flares his nostrils, and reluctantly follows Red Hawk's horse up the low hillside.

This is frightening country. A few trees dot the landscape in the distance, but it's basically a barren wasteland. I don't know how anything can survive out here. It's a curious revelation, for I have written that if the Indians were not so indolent they would choose civilization and became farmers. Now it is clear to me this country will never be farmed. It's suitable only for wolves, badgers, and snakes.

"Wait here," Red Hawk says.

When he rides away, I do not wait. Fog rolls over the dead like an approaching army of ghosts. We trot our horses, and when he stops, I stop. He examines each frozen corpse, studies the clothing designs, then rides on. Is he looking for someone?

My teeth never stop chattering. It's cold here. Very cold. My horse's hooves crackle on ice as he makes his way down the trail cut by Red Hawk's horse. High above us, fifty blue-coated soldiers have lined out on the ridge top, standing guard.

"Red Hawk, why weren't these bodies buried along with the others in the mass grave?"

"There was a bad blizzard. The burial detail didn't have time to search for more."

Windrunner tosses his head and shies away from a body. I can't make out whether it's male or female. I ride out the tantrum and guide the gelding back to Red Hawk's side. He does not seem to see me. He has eyes only for the dead.

I am happy with that. I do not wish to be seen today. I will only be able to truly observe when no one is looking, for I must silence my conscience. Eyes upon me change things. Especially Red Hawk's eyes. When he looks at me, I am afraid. I don't wish to see him. If I don't recognize him for what he is—an angry Indian—then his presence changes nothing.

Red Hawk quietly says, "Do you see the crushed fox burrow there on the ground between the dead children? Five kits were born a month ago. They should not have been born so early, but they were. They were helpless. Crazed men on horses thundered across the ground and buried them alive."

My eyes narrow. I have no idea why he told me that. Does he think I care about a den of dead foxes?

"Why do you care?" I ask.

"Look. Open your eyes. Try to understand what you are seeing."

I guide my horse over to stare down upon the crushed burrow surrounded by four frozen little boys. Five to ten years old, maybe. They lie on their sides with their ears to the ground.

Red Hawk says, "The children could hear the tiny foxes screaming beneath the soil as they died."

I glance at him. "That seems unlikely. Surely the kits must have been killed instantly."

"Nothing dies instantly. Not even when its head is cut off. The eyes still see for a time."

He dismounts and leads his horse around to the smallest boy.

"What…"

Red Hawk palms the air to say *be quiet*.

I close my mouth.

When he rises to his feet, he exhales a white cloud and then points. "The youngest boy died last. He had to watch his older brothers die before him. Do you think he called their names? Begged them for help?"

I study the corpses, wondering how he could possibly know the youngest boy died last. The child is maybe five years old. He has one arm out, apparently reaching for the brother closest to him. Leaning out of my saddle, I study the bullet wounds. The littlest boy was shot in the belly. The others were chest shots. I suppose he may have died last.

Red Hawk says, "It took hours for him to die. After his brothers were gone, do you think he begged the baby foxes for help?"

The question seems ridiculous. It makes me uncomfortable.

I look away. The other journalists have already arrived at the bottom of the hill, and with notebooks in hand, begun interviewing the soldiers who were present at the fight.

Red Hawk mounts and veers wide, leading me in an arc around the periphery of the battlefield. He is breathing hard.

"Can't we ride straight down to where the other journalists have gathered?"

"I do not wish to accidentally trample a tiny body hidden beneath the snow."

"Oh. I understand. I don't wish to either."

We continue riding in single file. It occurs to me that here at the far edges of the battle there are only women and children. Why would that be?

Red Hawk reins his horse and studies a woman's body. She was obviously shot in the back. Clotted blood froze around the wound. He dismounts quickly and kneels beside her. As though it requires herculean effort, he reaches out, grips her shoulder, and rips the body from the frozen grass to turn her over.

While he stares into her ghastly frozen eyes, I glance up at the soldiers on the ridge. Bits jingle as the animals shake their heads, disturbed by the scent that wafts on the wind. Closer to the journalists, Sioux scouts and police talk in low voices. Some weep.

I dismount and go over to where Red Hawk kneels.

He pets the woman's frozen hair. "My sister."

"I am sorry."

He looks at me with an expression of unmistakable agony. For the first time, I realize that the soul of a Sioux might possibly in its primitive state have started out on the same road as the soul of a white man.

Red Hawk moves to the bodies of the three children. Their arms and legs have frozen into macabre shapes. Their hands could be misshapen claws. One by one, he tenderly brushes the snow from their faces and smothers sobs. When he can look up at me, his lips quiver: "My nieces and nephew."

Bending over, he kisses their frozen faces, then his mouth moves in what I assume is a silent prayer. In spite of his shabby warrior's outfit, he's handsome in a swarthy sort of way, save for the jagged scar about three and a half inches long that mars his cheekbone.

Red Hawk straightens, props his hands on his hips,

and squeezes his eyes closed for several long moments. "They were just trying to run away," he tells me. "After Sitting Bull's murder, they were afraid. They only wanted to reach the safety of Pine Ridge Agency. They thought Red Cloud might be able to protect them from the soldiers."

I look at the journalists surrounded by soldiers. White voices mix with the sound of faint Indian sobs.

"Why is your family so far away from the center of the battlefield?" I softly ask.

"They weren't killed during the battle. Soldiers hunted them down later."

"Oh, that can't be right." I hesitate, then I go ahead and say, "Captain Robinson told me the troopers loved Indian children. He said they had only killed and wounded them in the confusion of battle."

Red Hawk's face shows no emotion. "When the blue-coats shot down the men, the women and children ran. Some headed for the shelter of that ravine over there, but the Hotchkiss guns opened fire on them."

"But surely that was an accident."

He takes a breath and lets it out slowly. "Many were blown to bits. I can still see the butchered women and children lying heaped and scattered all along that crooked gulch. Those that managed to keep running were cut down by mounted soldiers."

"On purpose?"

He stands perfectly still for several long moments. "We returned here two weeks ago and rescued the freezing survivors who were still hiding. We searched for bodies, but the snow was too deep. Many are missing. Some will never be found. Because of the Hotchkiss guns. The big shells chewed them up."

Red Hawk walks back to his horse.

My jaw clenches. I must remind myself that while the killing of children is indefensible, the squaws certainly deserved it. I heard the officers talking yesterday. They said the women fought along with the men, loading guns for the warriors, and using knives and revolvers to kill the soldiers.

But...Red Hawk's sister lies facedown surrounded by her children. There's a bullet hole in her back. My gaze carefully searches the ground for any sign of weapons.

There is only a toy bow.

Wind whistles across the ground, stirring a haze of snow. Something distracts me. A scent of dry grass perhaps, or a hint of laughter coming from the soldiers, a fragment of song. Camping on the Old Campground? In some form, despair whispers.

I notice that the cold blue sky is utterly empty.

My hands twitch. Every journalist knows this rupture. One moment you are confident you know what happened. The next, you know nothing. That's what the notebook is for. Stop looking. Start writing. Tell the story. Let the words be the trampling hooves that crush their warm dens.

Small running footsteps echo behind my eyes. I hear sobbing.

My notebook is in my coat pocket. But I do not reach for it. Not yet. While I watch the other journalists huddle together, smiling nervously, joking with each other, my mind rests in a vast ocean of silence. The road imagined must lead readers through the snow. He who travels the road must know he will never return. The fear must be conjured from their own experiences. They must already own the rifle shots, the shouts, the children screaming in terror.

I pass a young woman torn apart by the impact of bullets,

then the overturned wagon where the soldiers must have hidden with that look in their eyes, and she knew to run. There's a rag doll. I didn't see it until now. It's almost invisible beneath the snow, clutched in a child's fist.

"Mrs. Dean, are you ready?"

"Give me a moment longer."

Red Hawk nods and looks away.

In the twisting fog, the rolling hills seem to float over the dead. Disembodied witnesses that watch and listen. They are the only witnesses that could not be killed by bullets. Or rage. Or hopelessness.

I blink and my vision shimmers with a crystalline brilliance. My eyelashes and cheeks are so coated with ice I can't see clearly. I realize my face has begun to take on the sparkling mask of the dead.

Slowly, I walk back and mount my horse. Windrunner prances forward as though eager to leave this place. Red Hawk kicks his horse into a trot. I slowly follow in his tracks, roaming the frozen dead, peering down into glazed eyes, studying mouths that gape in a last cry. What name did they call?

I have a child. I know the name.

Mother, mother.

Red Hawk slows to wait for me to catch up. When I do, he says, "Do you see them?"

My brows lower. "Who? The soldiers?"

He points with his chin. "Ghosts are everywhere. Waiting for their families to find them and take care of them so they can move on."

An eerie sensation climbs my spine. I have heard that Indians have an uncanny ability to sense the world of the dead. Does he actually see something I do not? The possibility frightens me. I've had problems with nightmares and insomnia my whole life. When I was a little girl, every night I glimpsed a grinning man standing in my closet.

Red Hawk rides off. I watch him join the other Sioux policemen who stand together near the huddle of journalists.

I dismount and turn Windrunner loose. He nickers to the other horses and happily lopes down the hill toward the herd.

As I turn around in a full circle, my boots crunch snow.

There are voices in the wind, voices I almost recognize. "Help!" "Where are you?"

They are not gone. Not disappeared from this earth. I see them everywhere, moving in the fog. Over there. A woman with a baby in her arms. Rocking the infant. Back and forth. Down the slope, a father braids his son's hair, smiling as the boy whispers all the secrets he'd never tell his mother.

I draw in a breath and hurry down the trail cut through the snow by the horses.

A shadow slips in front of me. Racing feet.

"Stop!" I cry. "Who are you? Come back."

The journalists and soldiers stop talking and turn to look at me.

The girl charges ahead, kicking snow high into the air, leading me somewhere. I follow her to a ghostly lodge and step inside behind her. It's dark and cold, but I see her collapse on a pile of blankets and pound the folds, searching for someone who ought to be there. But isn't. She buries her face in the fabric and hides her eyes. I see the hole in the back of her head.

My ears ring. A terrible, immeasurable sense of wonder swells my body and burns through my blood. They will call me insane and gasp over every detail of my hallucinations, feigning horror. They will thrill at what I write. They will ignore the body count.

Stumbling now, I rush through the lodge flap and charge headlong through the snow.

There is a hazy figure peeking around a rock at the bottom of the trail. All I see is a head and one hand on the rock, but it has red eyes. I can't make out any features. About one-third of the way down, I realize he does not have red eyes. His eyes have been cut out. The sockets are pooled with frozen blood.

Someone calls, "Teresa, Teresa," and terror fills me. The figure lifts his hand and beckons me toward him with a war axe. I am stunned by the intensity of his smile.

Have I stepped over some threshold that separates this freezing killing field from the land of the dead? Before I can think about it I hear a loud savage scream, like that of a wild animal, and at the same instant am thrown to the ground by a hand I never saw. *Get down! The soldiers are coming. The soldiers are coming.*

"Dear God!" a man cries and several journalists rush up the trail toward me. "Are you all right?"

In a few heartbeats, I am surrounded by chattering men. Someone grips my arm and helps me to sit up. "My dear, are you hurt? That was quite a fall."

"No, no," I stammer. "I am well. Thank you."

The snow near the place of the red eyes eddies in an inexplicable manner. I can scarcely describe it. It has a shape, which bends and curls, as though being born into something new. A face turns slightly toward me. I hear drumbeats and singing.

I stare up. "Do you hear that?"

My rescuer looks around and shouts, "What?"

The other men murmur ominously. One says, "She's scared out of her wits. What's she doing here anyway? A female war correspondent. Ludicrous! I'm surprised she made it this long."

Right in front of me, a hand reaches up out of the snow, grabs my ankle, and pulls me down. A voice orders, Hide. Hide.

Panicked, I struggle to cover myself with snow.

Just as the women and children must have.

"She's hysterical! Find a doctor. Help! You there. We need a doctor!"

Two men haul me to my feet.

Shaking off their hands, I manage to choke out the words, "I do not need a doctor. Leave me alone! Get away from me!"

"See? I told you we should have left her lying here in the snow. Let's go."

Grumbling, the reporters march back down the slope, casting unpleasant backward glances at me.

A woman's voice is barely audible. *Run...run...*

I slap my gloves over my ears so I cannot hear her. As I stagger through the snow, voices pass by me, fleeing into the fog. The man with red eyes appears to my left and walks with me. His silence is more terrible than sound. His presence penetrates me like holy oil.

There is a special quality to this fear. Its heart is not terror, but abandonment, isolation, loss of meaning. I am dying alone, my lungs filling up with blood. I can't breathe. The Nicene Creed seeps through me: *I believe in things seen and unseen.*

My breath rises. Every step, every moment, I kill Isaac.

When I stand alone beneath the towering ridge, I pull my notebook from my coat pocket. And my pencil.

The eyeless man fades back into the fog.

It takes a moment before I can clear my blurry eyes and begin writing. My fingers are stiff from the cold. The first words resemble a child's unsteady scrawl.

We're talking about cultural death. Forced assimilation. Do you understand? They were afraid. They died in the bloody mud and were buried by snow.

They were just trying to run away.

• • •

Author's Note: Teresa Dean would become a respected war correspondent. She would go on to cover the Spanish-American War, the war in the Philippines, and the Boxer Rebellion in China, and she would cover each with the same honesty and integrity she displayed at Wounded Knee.

Black on Black: Marshal One-Eyed Jack Black

A Short Story

By Ash Lingam

"Can't you hurry this up a bit? I hear they eat dinner in Hades at twelve sharp, and I don't aim to be late."

— Black Jack Ketchum, just before he was hanged at Clayton, New Mexico, on April 26, 1901.

This short story is dedicated to Clint Eastwood and the American Western film industry.

Man in Black

THE DUSTY STREET OF THE SMALL TOWN WAS NARROW—SO narrow that the three gunmen standing at the other end couldn't spread out to make themselves a more difficult target. The blazing sun was overhead, casting dark shadows over the gunfighters' eyes from the brims of their hats. Each man wore pistols on their hips.

Sweat trickled down their necks as the tension intensified. A tumbleweed rolled across a Kansas street, propelled by a stiff summer breeze, making a crackling sound as it rolled along. Just above the three armed men was a sign that read *"Gun Sight, Kansas: Population 400."* The *400* was crossed out, and someone painted *200* beside it.

At the other end of the street stood a single man dressed in black. His hat was tilted forward, hiding his eyes until he finally lifted his head and glanced toward the gunslingers. His eyes blazed, their sky-blue color shooting hot daggers at his opponents. His pistols, with white bone handles and the letters *J.B.* carved on the sides, contrasted with the black clothing he wore. His hands hung beside his irons, ready to jump into action at the slightest twitch from the opposition.

US Marshal Jack Black had worked as a lawman for ten years, ever since he arrived in Kansas from where he hailed in the Arizona Territories. Kansas was in dire need of men to keep the peace. So. Jack Black was hired as soon as he arrived in Wichita. He was handy with his six-shooters and was given a US Deputy Marshal's job immediately.

He had crisscrossed the state, chasing down outlaws and putting an end to the lowlifes who chose the wrong side of the law. Kansas was full of men of reckless blood, lured by the money generated from cattle drives. Vast amounts of cash changed hands at the top of the food chain, allowing much of it to trickle down to poor folks and everyone in between. It attracted crooks and swindlers, who sought to charm earnings away from men, and thieves, who were more than willing to out-and-out take what wasn't theirs, be it from the living or the dead.

Marshal Black narrowed his sky-blue eyes until his eyelids closed to no more than slits, focusing on the faces of the three thieves. The outlaw in the middle swallowed. Black watched his Adam's apple bounce up and down. The marshal's powerful vision allowed him to see the beads of sweat form and run down the men's faces as they stood in the hot Kansas sun.

A door slammed, and some chickens clucked, but no other sound emanated from the streets of Gun Sight. All the folks in town had long sought cover from the imminent gunfire.

"Drop your guns, now!" Jack growled. "If ya pull on me, I swear I'll put ya down. Now, what y'all say?"

Time stopped. No one moved for what seemed like an eternity. Heartbeats pounded between the temples of the men as they waited for what was to come. Each dreaded the future. Someone was going to die.

Suddenly, Jack Black drew his two Colt 45s, cocking the hammers as he cleared leather. He pulled both triggers, sending two slugs of lead roaring out of the barrels as blood thundered through his veins. The bullets struck their targets at lightning speed, tearing flesh and bone on impact. Lead punctured vital organs and wreaked havoc on the bodies of the first two gunmen. They died instantly.

A fraction of a second later, another bullet spiraled out of the barrel of the smoking gun and struck the third outlaw in the head, just as he cleared leather. He got one shot off, but it buried itself in the ground. The outlaw took one step forward and fell to the earth, dead alongside his friends.

Jack stood there with his smoking pistols, keeping a keen eye on the men who now lay in the dirt. He was wary of being shot as one of them took his last breath. But the three bullets were well placed, as always.

Yeah, Marshal Jack Black pulled first, and the outlaws had to pay the price. Jack knew that three-to-one was no deadfall. He had to fire first if he wanted to come out of the gunfight unscathed. Dishing out death was what he did, a just reward for the crimes perpetrated by men on the other side of the law.

After a spell, Jack walked over to the three bodies and nudged each with the toe of his boot to make sure they had indeed passed. Dark pools of blood formed under each outlaw and mixed with the dust of the street.

Jack looked up at the saloon porch and saw the bartender peeking over the batwing doors.

"Ya best send the gravedigger over here with a wheelbarrow so we can clear this trash away before they start smelling up the whole town," Jack ordered.

The marshal confiscated the pistols and knives of each dead outlaw. He rummaged through their pockets, collected what they had, and looked for clues as to where they had been.

Next, he walked to the three horses tied to the saloon's hitching rail. In two saddlebags, he found some of the cash from the Gun Sight Savings & Loan robbery, but these were only three of the men involved. He was happy to retrieve most of the money before it could be spent.

Once Black had gone through their things, he untied their horses and walked them across the street to the livery. The caretaker, a tall, skinny fellow, was brushing a horse down but stopped to greet the marshal.

"That was damned quick when you throwed down on 'em, Marshal," the liveryman said.

"I'm surprised ya didn't run off like the rest of the folks when ya saw there was gonna be gunplay," Jack replied.

"I don't scare all that easily," he stated with a crooked smile. "I was bettin' on ya all the way, Marshal Black. I had little doubt you'd kill 'em."

"Well, I'm tough, but I'm fair," Jack replied. "I gave those boys a chance to give it up, but they chose not to take it. That's why they died."

"I reckon ya know that Jed's gonna come after ya for killin' his kin, don't cha?" the liveryman added.

"Who knows what the future will bring? We'll ride that horse when we get to it," Jack proclaimed.

He picked through his pockets, found a dollar, and gave the money to the liveryman, making the fellow's eyes twinkle.

"Thankee, kindly, partner," Jed replied. "Mighty generous of ya."

"You can keep those saddles as they ain't worth squat,

but I'll be takin' the horses with me back to Wichita," Jack said. Then, he turned on his heel and headed back across the street, where the gravedigger was waiting with a wheelbarrow.

"Well, whatcha waiting on, old man?" Jack asked.

"I can't get these big corpses into the wheelbarrow all on my own, Marshal," Horace Grim replied. "Gettin' 'em out is easy; it's the gettin' 'em up part I'm havin' difficulty with."

"You need yourself an assistant," Jack observed as he grabbed the boots of one of the outlaws, and together they tossed the first of the three into the cart.

"There ain't enough folks die around here as it is," he replied. "I can hardly feed myself. Due to your good law work, I'll be havin' me a decent month. If ya stick around for a spell, maybe ya could send a few more of these men of reckless blood asunder where they belong. I could use a little more business."

"I'll send out the bartender to help ya with the other two," the marshal said as he turned and headed for the saloon.

As he sidled up to the batwing doors, he peeked over the top to make sure there weren't any surprises waiting for him inside. Everything seemed to be quiet. Only about two dozen people were present, including the bartender, his helper, and three women selling their wares. All the while, the marshal had his hands resting on the white handles of his six-shooters. When he saw that no one inside presented a threat, Jack pushed his way into the saloon and over to the bar.

"What can I do for ya, Marshal?" the bartender asked. "That was some bully shootin'."

"It was justified. Give me a bottle of whiskey and a water glass," Jack replied in his gravelly voice. "You'd best send your helper out to assist Grim with the other two bodies. Those boys are a bit big for the gravedigger. Have you seen anything of the other two rascals that run with those outlaws that robbed the bank?"

"Oh, I saw 'em all right," he replied. "All five of 'em have been comin' here for the last three days. I suppose they were casing out the bank. It was just bad luck that you didn't run into the whole bunch all at once."

"Actually, it's a damned good thing I didn't because they'd have probably killed me. One of 'em got off a shot as it was. That's one too many for me," the marshal answered, his interest piqued. "Do you know where the other two gang members are holed up?"

"They seemed just to be driftin' from here to the other saloons and back. I doubt they've got themselves a room. The bunch seemed hell-bent on gettin' dead drunk. They could be just about anywhere by now, but if you wait right here, you'll more likely than not see 'em at some point. After they robbed the bank, none of the gang even left town. I reckon they are so stupid they thought they could spend all the money right here. Then again, they weren't countin' on a lawman like you, Marshal Black."

"Then ya better make me up a pot of hot coffee. I'll have a seat there at the table in the corner. And give me that towel, please. I'll give it back when I'm done."

The bartender busied himself, making some java for the marshal. Jack walked over to the table by the wall, pulled up a chair, and took a seat in the corner. Then, he plopped down, pulled one revolver, and reloaded. The second one got the same attention. He kept one loaded gun lying on the tabletop while he tended to the other in case one of the bank robbers showed up.

As the day went on, more and more cowboys moved in and out of the saloon. Jack still hadn't seen or heard from the remaining Stab brothers. The clan came out of New Mexico, and Jack figured it would be only a matter of time until they started looking for the rest of the boys in their gang. Of course, when they heard about the shootings, they'd probably come looking for Marshal Black.

Hours passed, and one empty bottle of whiskey and another nearly full bottle sat on Jack Black's table. He had his Colt hidden underneath the bar towel as he poured another half-glass of liquor and tossed it back. He clenched his teeth as the rotgut burned its way down. Jack was attempting to get rid of the bad taste his past had left in his mouth. The more he drank, the more his teeth ground. He was seething as he waited for the Stab boys to appear.

Finally, a voice called in from outside the saloon, and Jack heard two pairs of boots step onto the porch.

"Ya in there, law dog?" called Jake Stab, the eldest of the brothers. "I know ya kilt my boys, ya sumbitch. So, I'm callin' ya out here and now."

"You're gonna have to come in and fetch me, Stab," Jack roared. "I don't answer to the beck and call of outlaw trash!"

Jack's hands lay flat on the table, right next to the bar towel. The drink hadn't done anything but make Jack meaner. After consuming a whole bottle, the badger in him was awakened.

"I figure I'm gonna have to bring you down a peg or nine, Marshal Black," Stab shouted back.

"If ya keep on talkin', you're gonna talk yourself to death," Jack retorted, chuckling with confidence.

The double barrels of a shotgun blast blew the batwing doors off their hinges before the Stab brothers stepped inside. Jack reached for the bar towel, and his Colt-45. He raised the barrel and took a bead on the first man to enter. Jack shot him twice in the chest. The outlaw collapsed like a felled oak tree.

Behind him, charged the elder brother. He was a big man, powerfully strong and well spread out from too much food and drink.

Jack shot the man twice. It was like whacking at a bull with a fly swatter. His body jerked from the impact of the lead slugs, but he growled and kept moving forward. The marshal emptied the remaining rounds into the huge man, but he still didn't stop.

The elder Stab was so angry that four bullets had little effect; he just kept on coming, blood spilling from his face and chest. The twelve-inch blade of his Bowie knife hungered for Jack's guts. The marshal had never shot a man so many times with so little effect.

Stab charged toward the marshal, wailing like a banshee. It was the horrible and unmistakable sound of a wounded wolf, too full of pain to die.

Jack pushed the table aside, deftly slipped past the Bowie knife, and swung the spent Colt at Stab's head. The metal caught the wounded outlaw in the temple, and he dropped to the floor, where he bled out and died.

Jack pulled the black bandana from around his neck and wiped the sweat from his face. Then, he walked over to where the barman was cowering.

"You ever see anything like that?" Jack asked, still marveling how the man could continue his attack after being shot repeatedly.

"I've never even heard of anything like that," the bartender replied. "I thought he was gonna take ya with 'em, Marshal. I'd swear to it."

Texas Rangers

JACK SLEPT ON A JAIL CELL BUNK, WHICH WAS ONE OF THE quietest places in town. That was the main advantage of being located on the right side of Wichita. It reduced the noise from rambunctious cowboys in the red-light district. If the office had been on the town's wild side, his sleep would have been interrupted every hour by one altercation or another. Thefts and shootings were common but seldom reported because most drunken cowmen found the complaint unworthy of the walk across town. It would take them too far from the fun and their buddies.

So, when Marshal Jack Black wanted to have a spell of quiet time, he always knew he could find solace in cell number three. He procured a better-quality mattress and placed a chair next to the bunk so he could use it to rest his guns or sit and read by candlelight.

Today was one such day. The marshal had been dozing off and on in his bunk as he read about the Knights of the Round Table in England. He had a hard time imagining having to fight men with only swords and lances. Even the Indians had procured firearms. They quickly learned they had little opportunity for success against superior firepower.

Those would have been some hard times. Not to mention large-scale battles. The bloodshed must have been something frightening.

Three solid knocks at the door distracted him from his wandering thoughts and echoed through the empty office. Only one type of man would bang on a lawman's door like that, especially Marshal Black's office. It had to be a man with an attitude

"Who in tarnation is it now?" Jack growled from his prone position in the bunk, although he did reach beside him and grasped his Colt. While pulling back the hammer, he swung into a sitting position and rested his pistol on top of his thigh.

"It's Texas Ranger Captain Rowdy Bates," called the man from outside the door. "Is it safe to come in, Marshal Black?"

Jack got to his feet, ending his siesta, and quickly rummaged his memory for a face to put with the name Bates. He found nothing.

"I ain't gonna shoot as long as ya don't have a pistol in ya hand," Jack called out. "So, come on in already."

The Texas Ranger pushed the heavy timber door in. He poked his head and beige hat around the corner and grinned.

"I was told ya don't take kindly to bein' interrupted when you're havin' a siesta. So, I apologize for the interruption. Being I've come all the way from Laredo, Texas, I reckon it ain't too big an issue to lose a little sleep for a needy Texas Ranger, is it?"

"Unfortunately, outlaws don't work on my timetable. So, I adapt accordingly," Jack said with a smile. He took a sudden liking to the young Texan. "Come on in. I ain't gonna bite. Have a seat and tell me what it is you need."

As Jack looked the man over from head to toe, he saw a youngish captain, which indicated the man was no daisy. He was nearly Jack's height and even had blue eyes, Like Jack. His were a deeper, darker blue. His brown hair was pushed back on his head and slicked down with wax. He wore two pistols, set up for right-hand shooting. So, Bates was probably only proficient with his left hand. He had so many teeth that it looked like he had a cob of corn in his mouth when he smiled. He wore silver spurs on his boots and stood with an arrogance only found in young Texas Rangers.

"I'm after a horse thief, Marshal," the Ranger replied.

"So, since when does a Texas Ranger captain go hunting down one miserable horse thief? You'd think y'all would have enough recruits to take care of something like that. I thought your kind would be out fighting Comanche and all."

"Yeah, well, normally you'd be right," Bates replied, realizing Black had quickly discovered the chink in his armor. "Ya see, one of the four horses the thief took was mine. I ain't ever had anybody manage to steal my horse. So, I intend to find the villain and hang the sumbitch myself."

Jack tried to stifle a chuckle when he realized the young captain's predicament, making Bates jump to anger. He was unable to hide his irritation.

"Now take it easy, partner," Jack said with a smile. "I ain't making fun of ya or nothin'. But you've gotta admit, it is fairly humorous with you being a Texas Ranger and all. All that reputation didn't do much to deter a horse thief. Ya got a name for this outlaw?"

"Yeah, I got a name. He goes by Teddy Bundy. He was

hanging around Laredo for a spell. I knew he was up to something. Before I could figure out what, he stole the four best horses we had. He drugged the night guard with an opium-laced liquid and walked off with the horses, all of which have the Ranger brand on 'em. He stole a saddle that was mine, too. It'll say "Texas Rangers" at the bottom with my name on it.

"It was just my luck to lose my horse. Ya see, bad luck always comes in threes. First, I broke my knife. That itself was the darndest thing. I was playing Mumblety-peg, and the end just snapped off. Must have hit the dirt just right to break like that. I'd had that knife for the better part of ten years. Then, my dog got sick. He ate some loco weed, and it liked to kill 'em. But he survived. The third thing to go wrong was having my horse stolen along with the others. I'm hoping everything works itself out, and I find the horses before he sells 'em."

"There ain't no livery stables around here that will tend to government horses if the owners ain't with 'em," Jack assured the Ranger. "Unless, of course, he took them to the other end of town. For enough money, the stables on the way out of Wichita may do somethin' like that. I reckon if you want to look for your horses, we'd best start there."

"Well, I'm ready if you are, Marshal," Rowdy Bates said. "I would like to finish this up and get my horse and saddle back. Then I'll rest up for a day or two and head back down to Texas."

Jack stood, slipped his Colt into the holster with his other pistol, and strapped on his gun belt. He was ready to go to work. Black looked in the mirror, flicked his hair back from around his face, brushed the ends of his mustache with his knuckles, and put his hat on his head. He grabbed the brim, adjusting it to his liking.

"Let's go!" Jack said as he headed for the door. "Shouldn't be too hard to find your horses. Not with those brands on 'em."

"If I had caught up to the sumbitch in Bridge Town, Texas, it would have saved me a passel of ridin'," the young Ranger said. "But the rascal slipped out of town as soon as he heard I was there. So, I headed north, and here we are. I reckon he figures he can sell the horses to some unsuspecting cowboys or ship them east. But they'd have to modify the brands. It'd be too easy for 'em to get caught if they didn't."

Ten minutes later, the lawmen were standing in front of the last livery stable in the city. It was a rundown operation that had been rumored to buy and sell stolen animals on occasion. The man running the operation was careful and had never been caught.

"Howdy, Mr. Hancock," Marshal Black said when the owner of the stables walked out of the barn door.

"What y'all want around here? I ain't broke no laws," Handcock asked defensively.

"What makes ya think we're here makin' accusations?" Jack asked. "Maybe we just come by to buy a horse from ya. Let's go have a look at your stock."

"I ain't got nothin' to sell ya lawmen," Hancock stated, immediately making both the Ranger and the marshal suspicious.

Captain Bates wasn't having any of his stalling. He grabbed the man by the scruff of his collar and gave him a good tooth-rattling shake. He pulled his face close to his and growled, "If you don't give me the man who stole those horses, you ain't gonna walk away from this, mister. I've ridden a long way, and I'm just about out of patience. So, I'm gonna ask you one time. Where's Bundy stayin'?"

The man's pupils stretched wide with fear. So, Bates gave him another hard shake and pushed him away. The stableman wiped the spittle from his face, slumped his shoulders, and sighed before making his admission.

"Okay, Ranger. The horses are out back in the corral with the rest of the animals, and this Bundy fella has been stayin' in the whorehouse across the street for the last two days. I reckon he'll have the money spent in short order at the rate he's goin'."

"And that'll be unfortunate for you, mister," Bates snapped. "You ought to know better than to trade in stolen property. What's done with you will be up to Marshal Black, but I'll be tendin' to Bundy personally."

"Let's go have a look at those horses first. Make sure you ain't gonna shoot the wrong man," Jack chuckled, and got another cross look from the Ranger.

It didn't take but a few minutes to find the missing horse flesh, especially with one of the horses being the personal property of Captain Bates.

"Have we seen enough for you?" Bates snapped.

"Okay, I'll go with ya. I know the madam of the establishment. Maybe we can settle this without getting any citizens shot or wounded," Jack said and snickered again.

Bates turned on Black and asked, "What in the hell is the matter with you, Marshal? Why do you find me losing my horse funny? If you were in my boots, I reckon ya wouldn't be laughing."

"I apologize, Captain. I seldom see the humorous side of things, but I happen to find you to be a funny man. No offense intended."

That riled Bates even more. He saw nothing amusing about the situation.

"From where I'm standin', I don't see a damned thing funny about my belongings being stolen," Rowdy said. "Stealin' a man's horse and saddle is a hangin' offense."

"Well, I can understand that," Jack said, slow-like. "But from where I'm standin', it is somewhat humorous just the same."

Next, the two men walked across the street to where Madam Bluebonnet had her pleasure palace. When they got near the front door, they could smell the patchouli oil from the ladies of the night.

As soon as they showed up at the door a large, spread-out woman walked forward to greet the lawmen with a smile and sparkling eyes.

"Howdy. Marshal Black," she said with a grin. "Ya comin' over to have a good time with the ladies and maybe some poker? Or are you two handsome lawmen lookin' for some outlaw or other?"

"I'm afraid we are hunting for a horse thief, and we were told he's been in your establishment for the last two days," Jack explained. "The man goes by the name of Bundy."

"Why, that *is* a shame," she replied with a wicked smile. "He's been spending money like it was goin' out of style. Can't ya leave him to me until we get all his cash?"

"I reckon that'll be up to Captain Bates here," Jack said and again chuckled. It provoked another look of anger from the Texan.

"If ya don't cooperate with me, ma'am, I'm afraid I might have to roust all of your guests," Bates snarled. "I doubt ya wanna lose all your customers for some lowdown, thieving sumbitch."

"Well, now that you've made your point so clear, you can find the man you're looking for in room number eight. It's just up the stairs, the fourth door on the right. Do me a favor, though. If you have to shoot him, please do so outside. There ain't nothin' worse for business than gunplay and a dead body lying about."

Bates stormed across the room and shot up the flight

of stairs like a coyote was on his tail. His eyes were wide with anger, and his mouth was a thin line. He stormed into he room and captured the thief without firing a shot.

Instantly, Bundy began shouting and begging. Jack and the madam heard every word. The outlaw's protests ceased as suddenly as they started when the two showed up at the head of the stairs.

Bundy staggered down the stairs, bleeding. He had a deep gash over his temple with a cut down the side of his face. Captain Bates had already confiscated his sidearm and applied heavy handcuffs to his wrists. A chain teth-ered the handcuffs to the Ranger's belt.

"You're not takin' any chances on losing this one again, are ya?" Jack snickered. "Why don't we lock him up in one of my cells and notify the judge? Then, we can hang him all proper like in the morning. I can't let ya just hang a man in the street without some formality here in Wichita. Mind you, I ain't sayin' ya can't hang the outlaw, as he deserves it. We just don't want it to look like an act of vigilantism. This ain't Texas! Although ya got good call to detain the man, we have to go by Kansas laws."

You could see Rowdy rummaging around in his mind for a strong protest, but he couldn't find a valid one. The marshal was right. He had every right to arrest Bundy, but he couldn't kill him right off unless he threatened someone's life. It really didn't matter whose horse he stole.

"Fair enough, Marshal," Bates replied. "I can under-stand that. I caught 'em, and that's all that counts. Justice will be served, even if it isn't here and now."

"When you two handsome fellas get done locking up this outlaw trash, come on back. I'll buy ya two a bottle of whiskey for not shooting up the place," Madam Blue-bonnet suggested with a smile and mischievous twinkle in her eye. Hoping to replace one client with two more, the woman never let the opportunity to earn a dollar pass her by.

Once Teddy Bundy was locked up in cell number one, the lawmen walked back across town to Madam Bluebonnet's. Bates had had time to cool off some and was slowly taking to the town law.

"So, why is it ya wear all black, Jack?" Rowdy asked with a grin. "Is there more to it than being your name?"

"I did it at first because I was mourning the loss of some loved ones. Then, I figured it made me look more serious, black bein' the color of death and all. Now it's just become a habit. Folks who have heard of me can spot me quickly."

"I figure that could be a good thing, but then again it could be a bad thing, too," Rowdy said with a chuckle. "Flaunting who ya are makes ya easy to spot and shoot."

"Be that as it may, I have no plans to change my ways now," Jack replied. "I require a whiskey, so let's get a move on. I don't like being parched. I figure if I'm lucky, there'll be some boys shuffling a deck of cards. You feelin' lucky, Rowdy? Maybe what ya need is somethin' to take your mind off all that pent-up anger."

"Oh, I don't carry any anger or hate for my fellow man —even if he's surly, tiresome, and tries to cheat at cards," Rowdy said. "That's just human nature for a fella this far west. And he who calls for violence and dismay should have known better."

As soon as the two men walked back into the saloon and brothel, Jack noticed all the women had their eyes on them. Three ladies stepped forward as soon as he crossed the threshold. Always a ladies' man, Rowdy was unable to resist a good-looking woman. His eyes twinkled with delight.

Having saved his honor by retrieving his horse and saddle, it was time for the young Ranger to enjoy himself for the rest of the evening. And he did. The last time Black saw the humorous young Texan, he was surrounded by a blonde, a brunette, and a redhead, all beauties in their own right, fighting for time with the handsome lawman.

When Jack arrived back at the office, the only sound was the snoring of the soon-to-be-hanged horse thief. Jack never did understand how men sentenced to death could sleep or eat the night before they were to be sent to their Maker. Nonetheless, Bundy, who would hang first thing in the morning, was sleeping as if he didn't have a care in the world.

Jack walked over to the cell with a sly grin on his face and grabbed a tin cup on the way. He stood before the sleeping outlaw and ran the metal vessel along the bars, making so much racket Bundy nearly fell off his bunk.

"How's that livin' the life of an outlaw working out for ya there, Sparky?" Jack asked.

"Go to hell, Marshal!" Bundy said as he swung his legs off the cot and sat up with his feet on the floor. "I was having myself a nice sleep until you rudely woke me up."

"You best be pondering on what ya did and where you're headin', thief," Jack spat. "We plan to hang ya in just a few hours. I ain't here to see that your last days are happy ones. I'm here to dole out justice."

Finally, Jack headed for cell number three and rested with his boots on and his Colt cocked and lying beside him on the bed. The gun belt with his other revolver hung from the back of the chair, within reach if required.

Black was up just before daybreak, working on a fresh kettle of extra-strong coffee and frying pan biscuits and pork. The salty brine sizzled in the skillet, and the aroma of the bacon filled the room, making the lawman's mouth water.

"You got any of that food extra for me?" Bundy asked. "It smells mighty fine, Marshal Black."

"So, all of a sudden, you're feelin' friendly now that ya want somethin'?" Jack said with a snide grin.

He was interrupted by three solid knocks on the door. Captain Bates shouted, "I'm comin' in, Marshal. Don't shoot."

When the young Texas Ranger walked into the room, he was all smiles despite bloodshot eyes.

"Did Madam Bluebonnet show ya a good time, Rowdy?" Jack asked.

Captain Bates grinned from one ear to the other. "I reckon I had a fine time, and it worked all the mean right out of me."

"Does that mean you've had a change of heart and intend to let our horse thief live this morning?" Jack asked with mischievous eyes.

"Hell no! If it weren't for this piece of outlaw trash, I would have spent all day today at Bluebonnet's fine establishment. I just came back to see this sumbitch swing. Of course, I'll have some of that breakfast you're cookin' up. It sure does smell inviting."

"Well, grab yourself a pie tin from the shelf over there and a tin cup. Help yourself. I made enough for both of us."

"What about me?" the outlaw whined. "I got my rights to a last meal."

"When you stole the horses of the Texas Rangers, you forfeited all your rights," Captain Bates snarled.

Jack and Rowdy dug in and topped off the breakfast with coffee laced with whiskey.

"It's a little early to be drinkin', ain't it, Marshal?" Rowdy asked.

Jack looked down his nose with his two sky-blue eyes

and said in a gravelly voice, "And who are you to talk? You've been drunk all night."

"Yeah, but for me, it's still last night. I ain't been to sleep yet," the Texas Ranger laughed.

"You worry about your drinkin', and I'll worry about mine," Jack retorted. "We best get this grub cleaned up so we can get Mr. Horse Thief here ready to climb the hangman's scaffolding."

Peace & Quiet

It was a beautiful day in Wichita. The birds twittered in the trees, and a light breeze rose with the sun and moved across the country. The town was waking up, and suppliers were moving from their warehouses to the various establishments within the city. There was an array of businesses along the street—the Southern Opera House, Railway Eating House, Windsor Hotel, the Dallas Exchange Hotel, Wichita Valley Mill, and the US Marshal's Office, the headquarters of one Jack Black.

All these signs were indicative of a financially healthy city. The other side of town was populated with hotels, saloons, gambling halls, and pleasure palaces. All were crowded with cowboys day and night. This early in the morning, many were sound asleep alongside buildings, in alleyways, and on porches. Others hadn't stopped partying, mainly men who had toiled night and day driving herds of cattle north from Texas to Kansas. Once they delivered the cattle, a train took the beeves by the millions to New York, Boston, and other eastern destinations.

Between jobs, Marshal Black spent most of his time

in the local saloon drinking whiskey. He got more ornery with each drink, and today was no exception. He was a man with a badge, a set of guns, and a dark, tormenting past. It was a volatile combination. But the marshal directed his anger toward Kansas outlaws. So, nobody complained about how he did his job. The only thing local citizens saw was the lawman collecting prisoners. Most got shot or hanged, and it was as simple as that.

As Jack sat in the corner nursing his whiskey, in walked a fella who stood out even in this circus-like environment. His eyes bulged like there was too much pressure on his bumpy head. His face was grooved with wrinkles from forehead to chin. His mouth was twisted in a perpetual grimace. The man's nose was long and bent to one side, and he hunched his shoulders. Yes, the fellow was as ugly as homemade sin.

The unsightly gentleman looked around the room, letting his eyes move from one face to another until they landed on the tin star of the marshal. As soon as he set eyes on the lawman, he lurched his way, dragging his dopy leg as he scraped it across the saloon floor. Jack looked at the character, downed the whiskey that remained in his glass with one gulp, and frowned.

"Marshal?" he called out. "They told me to look for a man dressed all in black with a tin star pinned to his vest. It's Marshal Jack Black, ain't it?"

Jack Black nodded his head while holding a steady gaze on the man. "And you are?"

"The name is Kyle Bulldogger," the man replied.

Despite his uncomplimentary appearance, the man was clean and didn't offer any unpleasant odors.

He dragged his leg over to where Jack sat and said, "They've killed my kin and stolen the women!"

"Hostiles?" Jack shot back.

"No, sir, worse," the ugly man replied. "Slave traders."

Jack's eyes widened, and his teeth ground. He grabbed the edge of the table, leaned forward, and asked, "Where?"

"Just a half-day's ride west of here," the man added. "Three armed men came at us in the morning, two on horseback and one driving a jail wagon. They already had a couple of folks they had stolen in the wagon. They shot both my cousins and stole our wives and two young girls."

Jack seethed with the thought of the young girls. Laura and Clair, his wife and daughter, were stolen by suspected Apache slavers, although he never found out for sure. The man's words brought up those painful memories from ten years back.

"Did ya get any names?" Jack asked. "And how come you're here and you ain't dead like all the others?"

"I was out tendin' to my morning personals; that's the which of why I'm still alive. It all happened in the blink of an eye. They rode into our campsite hard and shot my cousins. Then, they grabbed the womenfolk, and off they went with our horses. I came here on foot, which is why I took so long. With good horses, we can catch up with 'em. That jail wagon will keep them from making good time."

"Slow down a minute," Jack said in his raspy voice, brought on by a decade of drinking whiskey. He set his sky-blue eyes on Kyle and added, "We'll ride out an hour before daylight tomorrow. They won't be driving that wagon tonight without a moon, so I'll have four horses ready for us first thing. Are ya fit to ride, mister?"

"All ya gotta do is help me get up and on a horse. From then on, ya won't find me trailin' behind. That's a promise. We gotta get the girls and the women back before they sell 'em and they disappear into this vast country."

Early the next morning, the two men met at the livery stable. Four horses were ready, one pair saddled and two others on a string line. Jack carried a couple of canteens. His saddlebags had some coffee, hard-tack, and lots of bullets.

It can be hard to track a man on a horse and even more difficult on foot, depending on how good he might be at covering his trail. Following a jail wagon is a task anybody can do. The clear track of the carriage wheels allowed the two men to ride hard without losing their way. Old Kyle kept up and even ran out in front; he was desperate to rescue the women before they were harmed. He pushed himself to the limit.

The chase was a painful reminder for the marshal. He had tracked those who stole his wife and daughter more than a decade ago, only to fail to rescue them. Marshal Black may well have become a hard man because of his failures, but now he never shied away from running down wicken men or a pack of thieves.

"I see a dust cloud out front," Jack finally said as he pulled his horse to a stop. He turned in his saddle and removed a small spyglass from his saddlebags. In the distance, he could just make out the box on the top of a wagon.

"What do we do now, Marshal?" Kyle asked. "I don't even own a gun, sir."

"For now, you ride right behind me. And stop talkin', or they'll hear ya," Black ordered.

As he pulled his Winchester from its sheath, the lawman carefully walked the horses toward the slavers. Kyle followed closely behind. They carried on until a couple of hours before sunset, when the men who traded in human flesh stopped for the night. As they began building a fire and setting up camp, Jack pulled to a stop.

"Here, Kyle," Jack whispered. "Take the reins of the extra horses and wait here for me. When ya hear shootin', make sure ya stay put. If I ain't back after a spell, you skedaddle on out of here quick. And don't stop till ya get back to Wichita. Then tell the sheriff what happened."

"Ya don't sound too sure of things, Marshal Black," Kyle said.

"I aim to reap the wrath. So, pretty much anything can happen," Jack replied with a furrowed brow and a grim look of determination.

The US Marshal got as close as he could without being seen or heard, carefully guiding his mount as he advanced. It was just turning dark, and the slavers' fire burned bright with the damp wood puffing and popping. The shadows made the flames dance across the marshal's face as he ground his teeth in anger. He was winding himself up in preparation for an assault against superior numbers. The marshal's only advantage was surprise.

Jack focused his hearing on the camp. Despite the jabbering of the three child-stealing fools, he could hear the women and the children whimpering and crying.

"Hush up, or I'll close that yap of yours for ya!" one of the slave traders cried out to the caged women. "Y'all best be grateful we ain't sold ya yet. What's awaitin' on ya won't be pleasant."

The words made the marshal's blood pound between his temples. He slid his rifle back into the scabbard and pulled his six-gun. He grabbed the reins with his left hand and snuck closer to the clearing.

When he arrived at the edge of their night camp, he put the reins between his teeth and clamped down hard. He pulled his left revolver and tapped the flanks of his horse. With restitution in both fists, he shot forward like a Baldwin locomotive.

"Fear the wrath, you sons-of-bitches!" Jack screamed as he charged into the camp, kicking up a cloud of dust.

Marshal Black's revolvers blazed as he rode through the clearing flat out. Two shots found their marks, and a man in a sombrero and one with a shock of red hair were shot dead. Once he had charged through the clearing, he stopped and spun his horse around for a second charge, squeezing his horse's flanks with his knees. Both Colts spat fire and lead as he resumed his assault.

One of the slavers, a man with long, dirty-blond hair, had his pistol up and was taking a bead on the charging lawman. A bullet whizzed through the crown of Jack's black hat, sending it sailing from his head. He aimed and pulled both triggers, sending two lead slugs roaring toward the body of the last man standing. They hit the outlaw with deadly force. His body jerked twice and fell backward, dead before he landed in a puff of dust, face up.

Jack looked over at the jail wagon, and he could see that the women were terrified of him as much as the evil men who held them captive.

"Y'all are safe now, ladies," Jack said softly. "I come here to save ya. Kyle Bulldogger sent me. The danger's over. See this badge? I'm a US Marshal."

Kyle suddenly appeared at the edge of the clearing and was grinnin' like a baked possum.

"I thought I told you to stay put," Jack snapped as he fussed with the chain that secured the jail wagon door. "Come on over here and tend to your kin, Kyle. We can ride back to Wichita in the morning. But we'll tie the door of the jail wagon open so the women don't feel threatened."

"Whatever you say, Marshal," Kyle said. Eager to

comfort his family, he dragged his leg across the dirt like a slug. The women and girls rushed into the arms of the ugly old man, crying and hugging him in relief. To them, he was the most beautiful sight in the world.

Jack retrieved his hat and tended to the four horses while Kyle did the same with his family. The marshal also dragged the bodies of the dead outlaws off with his horse. Once he got the three men out of smelling distance, he tended to the fire and continued with the pork and beans the outlaws were cooking.

The next morning, Jack let the bunch sleep in as they recovered from their ordeal. It gave him time to dig graves for the murdered men and bury them properly. Each man, woman, and child took a moment to say a few words over the graves of their family. Then, he dug one hole for the slave traders.

He had intended to make them a sign or something saying who the outlaws were and what they had done, but there wasn't much to work with. Finally, he tied two branches into a cross, and pounded it into the ground with his shovel, marking the spot of three dead men.

One Year Later

THE US MARSHAL WOKE UP WITH A START. BEADS OF perspiration covered his brow. He opened his eye and stared at the ceiling from his bunk. He blinked several times until his vision cleared, focusing on the cracks in the paint. He lifted his right hand to his face, wiped away the sweat, and tossed back the damp top sheet. Then he pushed himself up onto his elbows and looked out his open cell door.

Finally, he sat up, swung his legs out of the bunk, and placed his feet on the cool floor. He wore a pair of washed-out red long johns. Jack reached over to his vest hanging on one side of the chair and removed the makings of a cigarette from the pocket. He built himself a smoke and popped the end into his mouth.

The old marshal stared across the office with his one sky-blue eye and then at the leather eyepatch that hung from a peg on the chair. He slipped it over his head and adjusted it so it covered the eye socket, damaged when an outlaw stabbed him with a fork. In his business you ran into all kinds and in a moment's distraction he let him get too close. That was the last time he let his guard down.

He fished a wooden match from his vest, struck it on the jail cell floor, and put it to the end of his cigarette. He puffed it to life and wondered if the nightmares would ever end. Life had indeed gotten much better since he resolved to accept the loss of his family so many years ago. It took him over a decade to finally set aside the deaths of Laura and Clare and turn his eye to the future.

Yeah, Jack Black was getting old, but he was far from dead. As long as his eyesight, reflexes, and smarts held out, he figured he would continue to wear the tin star for another decade.

He chuckled as he looked back at himself and the dashing character he made as a young man, always wearing black with his white bone-handled Colts and two bright blue eyes. He still carried the identical pistols after all those years. He had worn the same badge for nearly thirty winters.

It was true. When he was young, he became too hard. Then, the whiskey eventually made him too soft. He finally found his balance and became what he needed to be—a tough, no-nonsense lawman who knew right from wrong. He never took a bribe, and he was the man to come to if you had a dirty job to do. When Marshal Black got on the trail of outlaws, it was all over but the burial.

Jack shifted himself from his bunk and strolled to the chair. He plunked down and pulled on his britches and boots. Next, he looked into the small mirror that hung from the cell bars. He brushed his mustache with his knuckles and stared at himself. He was getting along in years, but he still had a few more in him before he was ready to call it quits. He was as fast with his pistols now as he was twenty years ago—and that was damned quick.

Pierce, Arizona, had been generous to Jack. The community had offered him solid employment with a healthy paycheck at the end of each month. Plus, he got reward money when applicable. He was still living in a sheriff's office and sleeping in a jail cell, but now he had a good job, had quit the whiskey, and even had a new sweetheart. It was much more than he had ever expected in his life before encountering Harold Stampede, the scribbler from back East who wrote about Marshal One-Eyed Jack Black in his dime novels. The writer had said that the outlaw that removed his sight from one eye did him a favor when it came to selling his stories. It made for a much more mysterious character, but Jack was used to the strange things his scribbler friend came up with.

That was something Jack had yet to decide if he liked or not. It was what it was. Up until then, his fame hadn't cost him anything, and it made the outlaws fear the wrath he threatened to bestow on them. The black leather eyepatch sure did make him look dangerous.

Jack pulled on his shirt, grabbed his gun belt from a peg in the wall, and wrapped it around his waist, adjusting it to his liking. Then, he headed to the stove and lit the fire. The fall in Arizona was ending, and the mornings were cold. Jack could see his breath as he waited for the kindling to take hold and the coffee kettle sitting on top to heat up. Soon, the room smelled of fresh java, and warmth began to radiate in waves from the pot-bellied stove.

Jack sipped from his tin cup and pondered on his past. The fact that he seemed to have a bright future now, having gotten his life back on an even keel, pleased him. It was Sunday, and Jack and Gloria were going to take the buggy out to the country for a picnic by the creek.

Jack finished up his cup of java and placed it in the

wash pan. Then, he grabbed his brown coat and hat, stopped to adjust his eye patch, and walked out the door.

The End

"Black on Black" is a short story about the early years of One-Eyed Marshal Jack Black. The crafty but lethal lawman is featured in six novels, all of which can be found in the Ash Lingam catalog.

Shadrach

A Short Story

By V.J. Rose

Shadrach

"AND THEN I SAID, MR. WOODWARD, I KNOW YOU ARE madly in love with me, but I just can't tie myself down to one man yet. Why half the men in Possum Neck have proposed to me."

I nodded, my mouth full of pins, as I finished putting up the hem of her new "town" dress. I got up from my knees and removed the pins from my lips.

"You can take the dress off now, Miss Trixie."

I helped her out of the new dress and back into her old one. With large wide eyes and pouty lips, she really was a pretty little thing, and I could see men proposing to her, drunk or sober. However, I knew her well enough by now to realize that Mr. Woodward, whoever he was, had dodged a bullet. When she was in a good mood, she laughed and joked and paid on time. When she was in a bad mood, she was hateful, spiteful, and getting her to pay was harder than finding dinosaur teeth.

Soup simmered on the woodstove across the room. Comfortable chairs rested behind us. Since the cabin was two miles out of town and surrounded by tall trees, there was no need to go into the bedroom for the ladies' fittings. As I helped Trixie into her taffeta dress, I caught sight of myself in the full-length mirror I had set up for my clients. Older than Trixie, my hair was still blonde with curls in it, and although I was not as curvy as she was, no one could call me a stick either. I gave a sigh. No use even worrying about that kind of stuff.

I smiled. "I'll have the dress ready for you next week."

She wanted to talk more about her exciting conquests, and just as I was coming up with a plan to get her to leave, Otie barked.

Otie barked at everything and everybody, but they all had a different ring. This was not the bark he gave when a client's buggy pulled up. I went to the door with Trixie at my heels. As we peered out, my heart did a flip flop.

"Cade."

I thought I whispered it, but a glance at Trixie's avid face told me I had said it out loud, and she knew exactly who I was talking about. I ignored her and ran to the man who looked like he was about to fall off his horse.

"Hush, Otie," I cried, trying to take in everything at once.

Cade was still the handsome man I married, with dark eyes that could look right through a person and never let on what he was thinking. He wore the same expensive clothes that marked him as a gambler, along with the same big diamond ring he called his ace in the hole, although they were all covered in dust collected from many miles of riding.

Cade's hair, dark and slick, now showed gray at the temples. He appeared gray all over, and as he dismounted from the horse, I stood ready to catch him if he fell, he looked so weak. He managed to get to the hitching post and tie the reins to it. He leaned on it, trying to catch his breath. I put my arm around him to steady him, placing my other hand on his arm.

Trixie, who looked excited enough to burst, backed up.

"I'll see you, Mizz Blanchard."

She turned and almost ran toward her buggy. She jumped in, and taking the reins, urged the horse on, spooking him enough to make him move faster than he had in ten years. Old Man Henry at the livery stable would be furious with her for abusing his horse, but gossip could not wait.

"Take me into the house, Lou," Cade said, his voice breathless. "I've got to lie down."

He made the steps and over the threshold with my help.

"What was that woman doing here?"

"I'm sewing her a dress. The townswomen come on Mondays after they sell their eggs on Saturday. The ladies of the night come on Wednesdays after they'd had time to rest from the weekend."

I do not know why I was blabbing all this to him.

"Come on, let me get you back into the bedroom."

Avoiding the easy chair and rocker, Cade asked, "Did you get the two hundred dollars I sent you? You didn't write back."

"Well, I got it, but I was in one of those moods where I was thinking about divorcing you."

Every time I got to thinking about divorcing Cade, he would send me money. Cade always had a sixth sense about what people were thinking.

I got him on the bed and began removing his boots.

"You won't have to now. I'm dying, Lou. My ticker is giving out."

I stopped pulling on the boot. "Shouldn't I get the doctor?"

"No, it's too late. Take my pants off, too."

If Cade wanted to be stripped down to his long johns in the middle of the day, he was sick all right.

When I finished, I tried to get him to eat something.

He shook his head. "You got any lime around here?"

Cade always had a reason for everything he said, so I did not question him. I replied that I did.

"Take the horse into the barn. Make up some white-wash and paint a white socking on one leg and a star on his forehead."

"Is he stolen?"

Cade breathed heavily before answering. "No, I won him in a card game in New Orleans. He's a racehorse worth a lot of money, and I had to dodge crooks trying to steal him all the way into Texas. I made it to San Augustine where I got sick. I managed to hide out there until I was well enough to ride."

I did not ask Cade if he had cheated. He might take a horse if he thought he needed one, but it was a matter of honor for him not to cheat at cards.

"That dog bark?"

"Yes, he'll bark at any stranger who comes up to the place."

"Good." Cade closed his eyes. "Let me sleep."

He cracked an eye. "Wear my jacket when you approach that horse. He's a little skittish around strangers."

"What's his name?"

"Shadrach. He can run four miles without even being winded." He took a deep breath. "Not like me."

Cade rolled to his side and tried to catch his breath. Reluctantly, I left the bedroom, putting his other garments in the washtub. In my shocked mind, all I could think was if he was going to die, Cade would want to be buried looking nice.

About to put on his jacket, I stopped and held it next to my nose. It carried a scent that brought back a train wreck of memories. I found myself almost overcome with anger. Coming home to die after years of being gone. How dare he?

Outside, I untied the horse, and sure enough, he skittered around like a nervous Neddie on his first buggy ride with a pretty girl. It took several minutes of sweet talking and stroking before I could lead him away.

"Come on, Otie. Let's get this prima donna in the barn."

After watering Shadrach, I found oats Cade had tied in a poke sack around the saddle horn and fed some to him. Feeling a little more kindly toward me, the horse let me remove his saddle and begin brushing him down.

"You want me to tell you about Cade, Shadrach? Otie already knows all about him, don't you, Otie?"

My aggravation at Cade should have made the horse even more high-strung, but for some reason, the sound of my voice calmed him.

"Sixteen years old I was. Sixteen and dumb as dirt. The only thing I was smart enough to do was not let Cade Blanchard get into my drawers. I could tell that Trixie a thing or two."

The brushing revealed a beautiful seal-brown coat. Muscles rippled across Shadrach's shoulders, and he had a deep chest that could have held a freight train full of air.

"He was so besotted; he knew the only way he could get me was to marry me. He had won this place in a poker game. Oh, he was going to quit the cards. He was going to farm; he was going to build up a herd of cattle and ranch. And, oh God, he was so handsome."

The tail had tangles and burrs in it that took some

time brushing out. Otie lay down in front of the barn door and watched the road.

"He tried. He tried for over a year. But he couldn't stay away from the rambling life. At first, he would be gone a month or two. I wanted to go with him, but he wouldn't let me. He said it was no kind of life for me. Then it became many months before he would return home. And the stories in the newspapers...."

I finished with the tail and rested my cheek against the horse. Tears ran from my eyes like they had a mind of their own.

"And then he didn't come home anymore. Just sent money every now and then." Every time I got to thinking it was time to cut my losses and become a divorced woman, I'd get a letter with a few hundred dollars in it, and I could not bring myself to do it.

I wiped my tears on Cade's sleeve. Blinking, I went in search of the lime. Nothing was going to hide the fact Shadrach was a thoroughbred, but maybe Cade hoped to fool an observer spying from a distance.

It took three coats of whitewash to get the sock looking somewhat natural. Shadrach had not liked it much, but he submitted to it. I thickened the whitewash considerably with lime to do the star, and it was a good thing, too. Shadrach would not have stood for that indignation twice. Standing back, I looked at my handiwork. It would not fool anyone for long, but it did make Shadrach look more like a blooded horse meant to race in small towns, rather than a thoroughbred used to winning big purses at large tracks.

Otie began to bark, and I quickly hid the paint bucket and brush. Walking outside, I shut the barn door behind me. Looking down the wagon-rutted drive, my heart sank.

"Sheriff," I said when he halted his horse in front of me.

"Mizz Blanchard," he said, tipping his hat.

His wrinkle-lined face looked as serious and troubled as a father whose daughter is late coming home from a dance. Was Cade wanted by the law?

"Talk in town is that Cade is back."

I swallowed hard, trying to make the lump in my throat go down. "Yes, sir. He rode in this afternoon."

"I'd like to speak to him."

I shook my head. "You can tell me."

He did not like that. He shifted in the saddle and leaned forward.

"Mizz Blanchard, Cade has managed to stay out of the pen by the skin of his teeth, but he's built up quite a reputation as a gunman. All a man has to do is accuse him of cheating and just act like he might be going for his gun, and Cade shoots him dead. There are always witnesses declaring it was self-defense, but one of these days, he is going to shoot the wrong man, and the witnesses aren't going to be so willing to stand up for him."

The sheriff paused, and since he was waiting, I nodded my head that I understood.

"Frankly, I don't want him in my county. And if the Texas Rangers get wind of it, they may tell him to leave the countryside. You tell him that for me, Mizz Blanchard. I want him gone."

My face blushed a furious red. Not from shame, but from anger. I took a hold of myself and answered as evenly as I could.

"He's a dying man, Sheriff. I'd be much obliged if you'd stop by the funeral parlor and tell them to make Cade a tight, well-built casket. I want polished oak, not no cheap pine."

He stared at me for a moment, trying to decide if I was telling the truth. He gave a small shrug.

"I'm sorry, Mizz Blanchard. I know Cade has led you a hell of life."

"No, he has not," I said with as much firmness as I could put in my voice. I had cried to Shadrach, but I was not going to cry to the sheriff. "He gave me this beautiful property, this sweet cabin, and he sent money home. And he never raised a hand to me in anger."

The sheriff nodded. "I'll tell the undertaker about the casket."

"Thank you."

That evening, Cade ate a little soup. I did not bother to tell him of the sheriff's visit. He had his own plans.

"Is Rufus Coltrane still alive?"

"Yes, his wife passed away here 'while back, but he's still here."

"He still race?"

I shrugged my shoulders. "I don't know. I imagine. You know all the Coltranes are big horsemen."

I was beginning to see where Cade was going. His next words confirmed it.

"First thing in the morning, I want you to ride Shadrach to the Coltrane ranch. You tell Rufus that horse has won every six out of seven races. Don't you take less than five thousand dollars for him."

"Five thousand dollars!?"

Cade did not bother to answer, so I said, "I don't want to leave you."

"I want that horse gone before someone steals him."

"All right, but it's a three-hour ride to the Coltrane place. And he might want to dicker for hours. I might not be home for two days."

"I'll be all right. Leave me some biscuits. And take the dog with you."

The next morning, Cade gave me further instructions.

"Have Rufus ride with you to the bank. Put half of it in the bank and bring the other half home to hide. I don't trust banks."

"You're mighty sure he's going to buy Shadrach."

"None of the Coltranes can resist a good horse. But they will try to bargain. Just remember what I said. Nothing less than five thousand."

Shadrach was not the easiest horse to ride. He spooked at everything, even though most of the time, Otie ran ahead to scare any snakes and other critters away. I had to fight to hold on to the reins, to keep him from jumping sideways, or running off at the sight of mourning doves rising in the air. After an hour, I was close to exhaustion. I could not imagine how Cade had managed to get him home.

Passing through a mott of trees, two men came seemingly out of nowhere and began to ride with me even though Otie barked furiously at them and Shadrach tried to bolt.

"Can you call off your dog, ma'am, we don't mean no harm."

They spoke civilly enough. They did not look like tramps. I told Otie to hush, and his barks became less ferocious. I continued to ride, though, and refused to slow down or stop. They kept up with me.

"That sure is a fine-looking horse, ma'am."

I nodded my thanks.

"Can you stop a spell, ma'am? We sure would like to get a closer look at such a fine animal."

Cade had warned me not to let strangers touch Shadrach.

"How about it, ma'am? You and that horse look a little peaked. Be a good time for a rest."

During one of Cade's earlier trips home, he had left

me a Colt revolver. I pulled it out of my coat pocket. Or rather, Cade's coat pocket. Either way, I cocked it and waved it at the two men. Their eyes widened in shock.

"Possum Neck ain't much of a town, but they don't take kindly to strange men bothering ladies. I can shoot you both right now, and won't nothing happen to me. You hurt me, and they'll track you down and hang you. Now git."

They looked at one another and came to a mutual decision.

"We're leaving, lady. Be careful with that gun."

They left with Otie standing in attack mode, growling and ready to tear into them given the signal.

"Good boy, Otie. Let's go."

I kept riding, and after I was sure the men were gone, I let out a long breath and put the revolver back in my pocket. I was not used to riding much anymore, and after another half hour went by, I felt all three of us needed a rest. Passing a deserted creek, Otie jumped in. He swam back out and shook water on the bank, sending it flying. Shadrach sniffed the water, almost appearing to stick his nose up at it, but in the end, he caved in and drank. I had filled him with oats before we left the barn.

Tired, but still feeling a touch unsettled, I did want to stay longer than necessary. Otie had the stamina of a young dog, and Shadrach showed the stuff he was made of, too. Neither faunched at being urged back onto the road.

About half a mile from the Coltrane place, I halted and dismounted in a shallow arroyo that still had a little water left in it from a previous rain. It was nothing more than a puddle, but Shadrach was getting into the spirit of the ride and did not make a big to-do over it. Otie lapped it up without a thought. I drank out of a canteen and scanned the horizon. Cade had told me that Rufus would want to see the horse run, and he had said to stop and rest somewhere nearby for at least an hour before riding to the ranch house. We were probably on Coltrane land now.

I led Shadrach from the arroyo and hobbled him in tall grass. Walking to a nearby tree, I sat down, pulling the revolver from my pocket and placing it in my lap. With my back against the tree, my eyes grew heavy, and I fought to stay awake. The stress of having Cade show up sick was catching up with me. My days were spent in a secluded cabin, bent over a Singer sewing machine and cutting yards of fabric. Needles and thimbles were my tools, not Colt revolvers.

Cade was walking toward me in the tall grass. He looked so grand and handsome in his expensive black jacket and white ruffled shirt. But that could not be right. I was wearing Cade's jacket. Otie began to bark, loud and persistent.

My eyes flew open with a jerk of my head. I stood up on shaky legs and had to place my hand against the rough tree bark to steady myself. Otie had his nose to a turtle, occasionally poking its shell, and barking at it the rest of the time. Shadrach had drifted some distance away. I looked up at the sun, but was unable to ascertain how long I had been asleep. Judging by the distance Shadrach had covered, it had been long enough.

Shaking off sleep and finding my legs, I went to fetch Shadrach. Otie saw me and abandoned the turtle. With the hobbles back in the saddlebags, I got in the saddle, filled with dread at the thought of having to do horse trading, something I knew nothing about, with an expert at it.

The Coltrane ranch house was prettily situated on a rise with the river behind it. Made of brown iron ore rocks and timber, it had an air of solid stability.

I had barely known Mrs. Coltrane. She was a practical woman who sewed her own clothes and many of Rufus's. He had the reputation of being fearless and rough, but liked and admired by his peers. And almost completely under his small, shrewish wife's thumb.

The Coltrane hounds saw us approaching and jumped all over themselves trying to get off the veranda. They set off loud howls that Otie returned. Men appeared out of barns and doorways to stare at me.

Rufus came out of the main house. I had not expected to find him at home, thinking someone would have to fetch him. His appearance shocked me. Not handsome like Cade, he had nevertheless always been a nice-looking man. Now his hair was uncombed, gray stubble covered his face, and his clothes were wrinkled and looked unclean. Seeing me, he smoothed his unruly hair back and put on a hat.

As he walked toward me, the other men closed in, too, standing in silence as they stayed a few yards behind, watching me.

He tipped his hat. "Mrs. Blanchard, what brings you here?" He turned and hollered at the dogs to quiet down. Walking forward, he helped me from the horse, smelling of stale liquor, further surprising me since he had never been known for that habit. Thankful I had rested before riding in, I was able to stand without looking like I was about to fall over from being in the saddle too long.

"Cade is home. His heart is giving out or he would have come himself. He wants to sell this horse."

I went into the spiel of Shadrach's virtues. As I talked Rufus went over the horse with such a critical eye, I began to get nervous.

He motioned his head to one of the men standing nearby. "Take the saddle off him."

The cowboy did not hesitate, but stepped forward and

began to remove the saddle. Shadrach shied, but I held on tight to the reins.

"Cade had me paint the star and stocking on him. He was afraid somebody might recognize the horse and try to steal him."

"What did you say the horse's name is?"

I had not, but I answered, "Shadrach."

Rufus nodded, still looking the horse over. "I've heard of him," he murmured.

It did not surprise me that he had heard of Shadrach. In the horse world, he got around.

Rufus ordered another hand to get a bucket of water and remove the whitewash from the horse's leg and face. I was not going to have Shadrach throwing any fits, so when he brought the water bucket back, I said, "Let me," and taking the wet rag from him, began to rub away the whitewash.

When I finished, Rufus ran his hands all over Shadrach and examined his mouth. Shadrach got skittish, but I was able to calm him with a word or two. Rufus turned to me.

"Will you let me see him run?"

I nodded, still holding on to the reins.

He turned to one of the men. "Get Pete out here."

This time, he put the saddle back on himself.

"Saddle come with it?"

I hesitated. Cade had not given me instructions about the saddle. For some reason, I did not want to part with it.

"No," I answered.

We stood in uncomfortable silence while we waited for the mysterious Pete to appear.

"Cade have a bill of sale?"

"Yes, it's in my pocket." I wanted to say that Cade did not steal him, that Cade had not cheated at cards to win him. But instead, I set my chin a little higher. Just let him dare to insinuate such a thing, I thought, but Rufus did not. Suddenly, I felt ashamed of myself.

"I was sorry to hear of your wife's passing, Mr. Coltrane."

He shook his head without looking at me, as if it pained him to talk about it. To everyone's relief, a small man walked up, his face browned by the sun. Rufus appeared about to speak to him, but changed his mind and turned to one of the other cowboys.

"Go saddle up Red Boy and bring him out here."

He took off without a word while Pete addressed Rufus.

"You want to race them?"

"Yes. Start them over yonder by that big rock and race to the post oak, turn around and do it three times. You'd better make pretty with Shadrach before he tears off and takes Mizz Blanchard with him."

I handed the reins to Pete, not unconscious of the fact I had become "Mizz Blanchard" instead of the more formal "Mrs. Blanchard."

Pete had a cross face that warned humans to back off, but he communicated with Shadrach in a way only a true horseman could. The other cowboy returned astride Red Boy, a beautiful slick sorrel that lived up to his name. Pete swung a leg over Shadrach and got in the saddle, taking complete control of the high-strung animal with ease. They rode out together to the large rock.

Horses prancing, holding them side by side, they said words I could not hear until they both hollered, "Go!" at the same time. I held my breath, refusing to look at Rufus. The horses raced together one in front by a nose, then the other. On the second lap, a strange look came over Shadrach, as if he sensed the objective. An expression of determination crossed his countenance that was mighty to behold. Breathing fire from wide nostrils, taking in air with that huge chest, he left Red Boy far behind.

I wanted to jump up and holler, to clap my hands and squeal in laughter. I wanted to turn to Rufus Coltrane and shout, "Cade said he had endurance!"

But I did none of those things. Maybe I had learned more from Cade than I thought. The horses came back, the riders flush with excitement. Pete dismounted and stroked Shadrach. Rufus turned to me.

"How much?"

"Ten thousand dollars."

I had to choke down the gasp that came up in my throat. Why had I blurted out that outrageous amount? I had intended on asking seventy-five hundred and work my way down to five thousand.

Silence struck every man there. I fully expected Rufus Coltrane to laugh and say, "Well, sister, that's a little bit too close to the moon," or something like that.

Rufus did not laugh. He looked at the horse; he looked at me. He looked at the ground and back to me.

"Will Cade take a check or does he want cash?"

I almost swooned. I had to swallow hard. My voice squeaked when it came out. "A check for five thousand would be fine. He wants the rest in cash."

Rufus nodded while his hands stood looking like a giant worm had just eaten half their boss's brains.

"And he asked would you please take me to the bank to make sure it gets deposited and then back to our cabin safely."

"Yes, ma'am." Rufus turned to his men. "We'll take the wagon. That big dog looks like he might give out from excitement before the trip is over."

He looked back at me. "If you want to come inside the house, Mizz Blanchard, I'll get the money together."

I did not think my shaky legs could make it up the steps of the veranda.

"If it is all right, I'll sit in one of those chairs underneath the chinaberry tree and wait for you there." I might make it that far without faltering.

Rufus walked with me to the tree and made a cursory dusting of the chair with a dirty bandanna before heading inside the house. The chair was a homemade wooden affair that was rickety from being left outdoors, but it held my weight when I sat down. Otie lay on the ground near my feet.

I did not know what Cade was going to say, if he was going to accuse me of being flirtatious and leading Rufus Coltrane on to get that amount, or if he would just take my explanation that the words had popped out of my mouth with no planning whatsoever. At this point, I guess it really did not matter what he believed.

Neither Rufus nor I tried to make conversation on the way to the bank in Possum Neck. I guess I was afraid if I spoke and said the wrong thing, he might change his mind. Or maybe I was just worried about Cade. Would he even be alive when I got home?

The teller was turning the closed sign around when we reached the bank, but seeing who it was, he opened the door. The bank president came out, all jolly like, and was thrilled to deposit Rufus's big fat check into the paltry account Cade had left there for some reason only he knew.

With that done, I asked Rufus if I might stop by the general store. I wanted to pay my bill and buy enough groceries to have on hand to feed Cade. There was always hope he might get better.

We rode back to the cabin in silence. I did not know if there would be a dead body on my bed or not, but Cade was sitting in a rocker on the veranda when Rufus halted the wagon. He looked at us, his face expressionless, and watched as Rufus helped me alight and remove supplies from the wagon bed. By this time, Otie considered Cade a friend and went up to lick his hand.

Rufus greeted Cade while helping me take the supplies inside. With that done, we walked back onto the veranda. Rufus stood holding his hat in his hand.

"Here's your deposit slip, Cade. He's a fine horse. Thanks for letting me have first crack at him."

Cade looked down and saw the five-thousand-dollar amount written on the slip. He looked up at me and raised one eyebrow ever so slightly. I gave a nod in return. I turned to Rufus.

"Would you like to sit down and have a cup of coffee?"

"No, ma'am. I'm going to head on. I might come by tomorrow and have a word with Cade if he's up to it."

A look, an understanding, passed between the two men that I did not comprehend. Cade only nodded, and Rufus left. When he was out of sight, I pulled out the money and handed it to Cade.

"I don't know what came over me. When he said how much did you want, I said ten thousand dollars. And he agreed. My knees almost gave way."

Cade handed the wad back to me. "Hide it in the flour barrel." He rose to his feet, every breath an effort.

After we walked into the cabin, I started chattering about how impressive Shadrach had been that afternoon as I wrapped the money and buried it deep into the flour. I turned, only to see that Cade had gone back into the bedroom.

I looked back to the flour, a tear sliding down my cheek.

The next morning, a cleaned-up Rufus came back, this time with two other men—a cowboy who worked on his ranch and the town's lawyer. The lawyer stayed on the wagon bench and the cowboy remained on his horse while Rufus got down.

He removed his hat. "I'd like a few words with Cade, Mizz Blanchard."

He did not really wait for a reply, but walked into the cabin and back into the bedroom, closing the door behind him. I looked at the other two men.

"Would you like to get down and rest a spell?"

"No, ma'am," the cowboy answered in a laconic voice. "We be fine right here."

Rufus came out onto the veranda and motioned for them to come inside. The cowboy dismounted, letting the reins fall to the ground. The little lawyer in his derby hat got down from the wagon clutching some kind of leather satchel. He straightened and followed the cowboy into Cade's bedroom.

I shrugged to Otie. "To heck with them," and went back to feeding my chickens.

When they came out, I was bringing in a bucket of water from the well. The cowboy grabbed it from me and took it into the house.

"Mizz Blanchard, you let me know if you need help," Rufus said. "I've spread the word in town that people aren't to bother you and Cade."

I thanked him, and they said their goodbyes without even asking for a drink of water or a cup of coffee. I wondered at Rufus's last statement. Nobody ever bothered me, and most of Cade's friends had drifted away.

Cade stretched flat on his back on the bed, staring at the ceiling when I walked in.

"What was that all about?"

He turned his head to me. "They wanted me to sign a will leaving you all my possessions so you wouldn't have any trouble when the time comes. The joke was on them.

I had already made one. There's going to be a lot of skunks and snakes coming out of the woods when I die, Lou.

"Come lay by me, sweetheart. I'm afraid to die alone."

It was like that two days later, when he opened his eyes, looked across the room, and said, "Mama."

I stayed with him, crying and holding him until his body grew cold, and I knew Cade would never be coming back to me again.

The day before Cade died, he had given me his ring. I put it on a chain around my neck. Now I dressed him in his clean clothes, making sure his face was shaven and his hair combed just the way he liked it. He had lost weight, but even so, I could not lift him. I made Otie stay in the house with him while I rode into town to fetch the undertaker.

On the morning of the funeral, Rufus Coltrane arrived dressed in a suit and sitting in a smart-looking buggy. He asked if I would like for him to take me to the funeral. I nodded, grateful for the company. I did not expect there to be more than a handful of people in attendance, but for some reason I had decided to wear a hat with a black veil covering my face.

When Rufus and I drove up to the cemetery, my mouth dropped open. There had to be at least two or three hundred people there—people from all walks of life. I turned to Rufus.

"I didn't realize Cade had so many friends."

"They are not friends, Mizz Blanchard. They are vultures come to see a gunfighter and gambler laid to rest."

I had no desire to get out of the buggy, but I allowed Rufus to help me down, nonetheless. I walked like a ghost of a woman—hardly breathing, unbelieving. Rufus and his cowboys pushed the crowd aside so I could reach the grave. The preacher saw me and began to speak, but I scarcely knew what he said. After a time, Rufus took my hand and whispered in my ear.

"They are waiting for you to throw a handful of dirt in the grave."

I did as he said. The scattering of dirt had barely settled when one woman began hollering and crying.

"Oh Cade! Oh Cade!"

I had never heard such squalling. I looked up to see a blur of rouged cheeks and garish clothes. Before I could even begin to sort it out, another woman took up howling and moaning—she, too, dressed as a tart. They turned their shrieks on one another and began to fight, scratching and pulling hair right in front of the grave.

Rufus began hustling me away. A man in a blue suit jumped in front of us.

"I hate to bother you at a time like this, Mrs. Blanchard, but Cade owed me two hundred dollars."

Two of Rufus's cowhands picked him up by the arms and physically carried him off.

Rufus continued to push people away until he could get me in the buggy. I could hear the women still screaming. Once on the buggy seat, Rufus had to use the whip on somebody who kept trying to grab at my necklace.

We raced out of town, wheels spinning and flying hoofs throwing dirt in every direction. I leaned forward in shock, holding my stomach, unable to cry, hardly able to breathe. After a time, the buggy slowed, and I sat upright, pushing the veil back from my face. It took a few seconds to realize we were not going straight back home. Rufus saw the question in my eyes.

"I'm taking the long way."

I murmured my thanks, not wanting anyone from the funeral following us either.

Rufus slowed the buggy down even more. This time, I wanted to talk.

"Cade tried to warn me. I just had no idea. And those women."

"They didn't mean anything to Cade."

Tears fell down my cheeks. Brushing them aside, I began to talk about Cade, about meeting him and our life together. Rufus was a good listener, and he kept the horses plodding at a slow pace.

After some time on the circuitous route, we reached the cabin. Rufus pulled up on the reins, halting the horses. Otie made a few happy barks but stopped to sniff the wagon wheels. Rufus tied the reins but made no move to get down or say goodbye. I paused, waiting. He spoke, hesitating over his words.

"Mizz Blanchard, Cade could not help what he was. But you were his rock, and having a good woman like you to love him back, well, it kept him from going completely bad.

"Those screaming whores at the funeral were just used to pass the time, not someone a man could ever trust his horse with."

His craggy face flushed red. "Pardon me, ma'am. Sometimes I use salty language without thinking."

Trying to keep from choking up, I answered from a wrung-out heart.

"I'm going to miss Shadrach. Maybe you can bring him by to visit one of these days."

"Yes, ma'am. I'd like that."

The End

Little Snake

A Short Story

By W. Michael Gear

Little Snake

It rained a lot after the Collapse, but then no one had ever said the end of the world would be pleasant. Now it fell in sheets that battered the windshield; the kind of rain that overwhelmed each swipe of the wipers. Nels Curley leaned forward over the wheel, the defroster roaring as it kept the windshield from fogging. The highway came off as a smear in the downpour, the road flowing with water. They said that it was a form of "nuclear winter," that soot from the burning cities and forests had filled the atmosphere to the point that sunlight just couldn't get through. And, on occasion, the folks monitoring the air kept a close eye for radiation.

All Nels could see was endless silver splashes on the leaden and ringed surface. Headed east toward Dixon, Wyoming, the reflector posts barely kept him on the asphalt.

He was a medium-framed man, early forties, with thoughtful brown eyes and the kind of face women called handsome. It had a square-jawed look accented by a mobile mouth and straight nose. Nels had to look good.

He served on Wyoming Governor Pete Agar's staff and often functioned as the governor's public face.

On a fact-finding trip for Governor Agar, Nels had been in the little town of Baggs, checking with the Second Quadrant commander, Major Tim Sakroy, of the Wyoming National Guard when the storm really broke.

"Yeah, we're worried about what's going on over in Dixon," the major had told him. "Got a so-called militia unit there that runs things their way. Glad the governor sent you down. My orders are to keep unauthorized people from entering the state from Colorado at the Highway 789 checkpoint just south of town. What goes on east of here is kind of like no-man's-land. I don't have the manpower or the motivation to stick my nose into it."

"Maybe I'll just drive over and see."

Sakroy gave him a "you're crazy" look. "I wouldn't."

"Governor Agar sent me down here to get a firsthand look. How do I know what to tell Agar if I haven't seen it to be sure?"

"Okay, but Nels, you get in a bind over in Dixon, I don't have the people to come riding to the rescue. You're on your own."

Curious stories were being floated about what was happening in the southwestern corner of Carbon County, the section of "The Line" along the Colorado border. Wyoming's colorful history was filled with stories about wealthy individuals and powerful organizations running affairs as they saw fit: the Johnson County war; the use of hired killers like Tom Horn; Albert Bothwell's infamous hanging of Cattle Kate and husband Jim Averell; and back in the day, the nefarious illegal high jinks by the Wyoming Stock Growers Association.

Now, as the immensity of the national collapse became clear, the old ways were once again raising their ugly heads. After the attempt by NSA Director Edgemont to take over the Big Horn Basin, Governor Agar had sworn there would be no fiefdoms, no personal empires established in the wake of the Collapse. The United States might have fallen, the East Coast might have been nuked, and hundreds of millions might have died when the lights went out and the food was exhausted, but Wyoming would remain a final if faint beacon of civilization.

Lightning flickered in strobes of white that illuminated the rain-shiny grass, trees, and ditches to either side of the blacktop. Here, the road ran along the Little Snake River floodplain; barbed wire fences lined either side of the right of way. Thunder cracked a deafening blast just over Nels's head. Made his heart skip. Wind thrashed the cottonwood trees with a violence that ripped big green leaves loose to dance away on wicked gusts. It slapped the Ram 2500 pickup's right side in a fusillade of battering rain.

Passing a family ranch, he could see the cattle, maybe thirty head, packed in a small pasture next to the weather-faded barn. They looked wet and dejected, heads down. Hell, the whole place looked miserable. But then, that was the world they lived in. At least these people still had animals that would provide them with food and trade.

When Nels reached the green highway sign proclaiming the Dixon town limits, he encountered two pickups marked DIXON MILITIA parked so as to partially block travel.

Nels slowed as the driver's door on the Ford F-250 opened and a teenage kid emerged to slap a straw cowboy hat on his head against the downpour. He came splashing forward, shoulders hunched as his worn Levi jacket bore the brunt of the falling rain. A scoped bolt-action hunting rifle hung from his right hand.

Nels rolled his window down, meeting the boy's dark eyes where they stared suspiciously from a thin face. The kid, maybe sixteen or seventeen, asked, "Who are you and what's your business?"

Nels reached into his jacket pocket and produced the governor's letter replete with the official seal. "Nels Curley. Governor's Office, Cheyenne. I'm on official business."

The kid stared at the letter, rain pattering on his hat so hard that it was dribbling through the weave on the straw brim. "That means...what?"

"You will let me pass," Nels replied. "Who's in charge here?"

"Um, that would be Major Hampton. He's, um, running the whole Second Quadrant."

Which would be news to Major Sakroy and the rest of the Wyoming National Guard back in Baggs.

Jagged lightning flashed a tortured white streak across the sky; it left Nels and the kid blinking in the second before the deafening crack made the kid jump half out of his now-soaked boots.

"Hotel still have rooms?" Nels asked, hating the rain that spattered on the truck's windowsill.

"Ask Sally at the bar."

Nels slipped the Ram in gear. Feeding it throttle, he pulled away, headed for the gap between the blocking pickups. As he rolled the window up, he heard the kid yell, "Hey! I didn't say you could go!"

Then he was through the gap. Not that there was much town to see. Prior to the Collapse, Dixon boasted about eighty people. The residences favored frame or modulars mixed among aging mobile homes. Most were set on tidy lots with large trees and neat yards. The senior center now sported a sign declaring TRADE MARKET and in smaller letters CASH PREFERRED BARTER TAKEN. The historic Town Hall had a sign in the window painted in block letters: Militia Headquarters. Major Dewey Hampton, Commander.

Nels turned on 3rd Street and pulled in at the bar next to a line of pickups. He was about to step out when—through the rain-slicked driver's window—he caught movement. Rolling the window down a crack, he could see cattle emerging from the side street. Mostly Angus, there were a few black baldies, some Hereford crosses, and to his surprise, a couple of Galloways.

At the head rode a young woman on a water-plastered red horse. Or Nels figured it was a woman given her slight frame and the way she sat the saddle. Details couldn't be made out since her sodden hat was pulled low and the slicker she wore hung like a tent. He could see her breath fog as she whistled and called to the cattle; flicking a coil of rope, she turned them east onto the highway.

At that junction, the bar door opened, and five men, donning coats, western hats clamped on their heads, scrambled to the pickups. Doors slammed. One by one, they pulled out, heading the half block down to the cattle drive. A second rider, a man this time, reined his horse around, trotting toward the first pickup. He pulled up and leaned down as the driver stopped and lowered his window.

Nels could just hear the called greeting. "Got 'em all back, by God. That damn woman's pure hell with that big rifle of hers. Killed 'em all. Never seen the like."

Any reply was drowned out by a rolling boom of thunder.

The last of the cattle were pushed out onto the road by a tall rider on drag. Another woman, if Nels was any judge. She, too, was tightly bundled against the rain, her hat drooping, slicker glistening in the gray light. Unusual, however, was the long, cased rifle strapped crossways on the skirts above stuffed saddlebags and beneath a thick bedroll. She led a packhorse with a mantied load tied in a neat double diamond hitch.

The woman gave the waiting pickups a dismissive glance before calling out, "Kai! Yip!" at a couple of malingering cows. She deftly cut behind, hazing them back into the herd that now lined out on the highway.

Nels clamped his own hat down tight, a custom O'Farrell he'd ordered a couple of years before the Collapse, and slipped into his coat. Then, stepping out into the rain, he splashed his way to the bar's door and entered.

Wyoming is home to some famous watering holes: The Cowboy Bar in Jackson; the Irma and Cassie's in Cody; The Beacon Club in Casper; and The Mint in Sheridan, and Mayflower in Cheyenne among others. The Dixon Bar fell into that august company. Stepping inside was to slip back fifty years into a different world. Those knotty-pine walls had witnessed a lot of history: ranchers, cowboys, fist fights, celebrities, and politicians, all leaving a ghost of themselves in the glow of the neon lights. Normal for a Wyoming rural bar with its pool table, dart board, and the cheap-upholstered stools lined before the plank-topped bar. Now only a few bottles remained on the backbar. And, of course, there were the scarred high-top tables and booths.

The woman behind the bar straightened from where she collected the glasses left by the cowboys and gave Nels a curious study.

In a voice that sounded like cigarettes and gravel, she asked, "Welcome. Been a while since we've seen a strange face. Who are you and where are you from?"

"Nels Curley. From Cheyenne. Governor's office. Here on official business. Looking for Sally Watson."

"That's me."

"What's a room at the hotel across the street go for these days?"

She narrowed her eyes, set the tray of dirty glasses next to the sink, and bracing on her elbows, stretched over the bar. "Cash?"

"Cash."

"If you're not bullshitting, I'll let you have a room for a hundred bucks."

"Fifty," Nels countered. "I'm on per diem."

"Show me the money."

He extracted his wallet, peeling out a hundred-dollar bill. Of course she wanted to see the money. Credit cards died the day of the Collapse. "Got change?"

Sally burst out in a throaty chuckle. "Get real. After the banks went down, cash is as rare as hen's teeth." A pause. "You here just for the night?"

"Depends." He studied the faded bill. "But how about this? You take the C note and think of me kindly."

The hard eyes returned to the suspicious slitted look. "How kindly?"

Nels leaned on the bar next to her. "Cards on the table? A lot of rumors are drifting out of this part of Carbon County. I was just in Baggs, and Major Sakroy, he's in charge of the Wyoming National Guard in this quadrant, says that even though it's only eight miles down the road, it's like a curtain's been drawn. Governor Agar wants to know what's going on."

"I'll bet he would."

"What's with the roadblock and that high school kid with a rifle?"

"Oh, you mean Rory Jackman? Typical high school

teenage boy. All hormones and no brains. Thinks manning the roadblock makes him a big man."

She studied him from the corner of her eye, reached out with two fingers, and snatched the hundred. "All right. I'm from here. Fourth generation. So I've got some roots. You know about Dewey Hampton?"

"Millionaire. Made his money in California tech. Came in about five years back and bought the Tapadero Ranch. Then he started buying up all the land he could along the Little Snake River. He was planning some big resort development up on Battle Creek. Got in a snit with the Forest Service and some of the locals who were afraid that Dixon and Savory would get the same kind of shafting folks up in Jackson Hole got when the billion-aires moved in. There's bad blood between him and Governor Agar."

She nodded. "That's him. After the banks failed and the whole country went to shit, good ol' Dewey stepped in and sort of took over. When Agar closed the border and called for a militia to back up the WNG, Dewey moved right in calling the shots."

Sally reached into a pocket, pulling out a cigarette. She glanced at it. Tapped it with a finger. "I have three packs left. Save 'em for special occasions since we're never going to see tobacco again in our lifetimes." She lit up, pulled, and sighed as she blew out smoke.

"Things got stretched pretty thin after the Collapse," Nels told her. "Nothing coming out of the east. Talk of Chinese on the West Coast. Then the Front Range communities down in Colorado tried to flee north and swamp us. Denver, Boulder, Fort Collins, Longmont, they're dead zones now. Burned out, looted, bodies left where they fell. So the threat's eased from that direction."

"Different here." Sally drew deeply, eyes closed in rapture. "Northwest Colorado's like us. Small communities, mostly agricultural. They had their own trouble with people flooding out of Grand Junction and Denver, and then others came drifting in from Utah. Took matters into their own hands. But they're hanging on. And they have the power plant down in Craig." She waved at the lights. "We still have electricity. Dewey sees that they get paid. Not sure how or if it's all barter."

"But?" Nels asked softly.

"Like I say, those folks down there are like us. Lots of longtime friends and family on both sides of the state line. Sure, that WNG checkpoint sits on the highway south of Baggs, and during the day, nobody gets across the line. What happens after dark's another thing. Same thing here, but Dewey Hampton takes a cut. And people who don't fork over a couple of calves, or maybe a five-gallon can of gas if they still have it, or don't offer a couple of days' work, or pitch in on one of the Tapadero projects?" She shrugged for emphasis.

"Bad news, huh?"

"Let's just say that those people you were talking about? The ones that helped kill that resort he wanted to build? They're all gone. Sometimes it was a mysterious fire. Or oddly, they just vanished one night, never to be heard of again. Funny thing, a day or two later, Dewey Hampton's suddenly running his cattle on their land." Sally fixed her hard eyes on his. "And we haven't heard jack shit from Cheyenne. Or even the county seat up at Rawlins. Like nobody gives a damn what happens down here."

Nels pursed his lips. "We've been a little busy."

"So, what's the good governor's game plan? And what's in it for us?"

"Saving as much as we can. We've got petroleum, and the refineries are still running. Power plants, food production. Our communities are intact, and we're working on medicine. Just recovered a medical lab from Colorado to make insulin and other meds." He pointed. "Given that tobacco-growing country has been irradiated back east, I'd hang onto those."

She smiled, took another draw.

"That cattle drive?" Nels asked. "Dewey's?"

She shifted, the sidelong gaze back. "Yeah. Dewey had a falling out with a rancher developer south of the line named Bud Carullo. Competitor of sorts since he was setting himself up to be a kingpin in northern Moffat County. Carullo sent a bunch of his riders up to haze Tapadero cattle off a Carullo forest lease. Ex-military, you know? It got nasty, and two of Dewey's riders were killed. The Carullo bunch took the cattle and some girl they had with them. Dewey hired a woman named Salva to get the herd back. She said all she needed was one guy. Took Danny Sexton with her. He's a top hand. Best cowboy in these parts. Folks here thought that was the last we'd see of old Danny." She chuckled. "And then, damn if Salva doesn't come riding in with the herd."

"Salva?" Nels asked softly. "Thea Salva?"

"Know her?"

"She was one of Edgewater's hired goons up in Park County. Sort of dropped off the map after his compound was raided. Word is that she's bad news."

"Whatever she is, Dewey's cattle are back." Sally pointed at the back bar. "But I got my own problems. Notice how most of those bottles are verging on empty? We got some local hooch. It's shit. So, does your good governor have a source for spirits and beer that's not swill? Maybe a source for food now that Sysco's gone?"

"We do. Most of the microbreweries and distilleries are still turning out product. And we've got potatoes from Idaho, sugar from the Bighorn Basin, gasoline, lots of stuff. Open for business."

"And only one problem," Sally noted. "Dewey Hampton will want to control it all." She straightened. "Let me get your room key."

Nels spent the few hours until dusk seated in the uncomfortable chair at the room's worn desk. He finished typing out his report of the day's activities and detailing what Major Sakroy and Sally Watson had told him.

The old impulse to send it off to Cheyenne as an email would never go away. The joy and curse of the internet and instant communication—along with cell service— had vanished in the wake of the Collapse. He saved the file. It would be downloaded and printed upon his return to Cheyenne. Pain in the ass, but his eighty-year-old father would have reminded him that all reports had been delivered that way back in the day. It just seemed so...primitive!

Nels closed his computer, slipped it into his briefcase, and tugged on his coat and hat before locking the room and walking to the second-floor exit. As he descended the stairs, rain was still falling. But that was the world after the Collapse. Constantly cloudy. Gray.

The rain beat on his hat and coat as he splashed across the road to the bar. A single pickup was parked out front; the red OPEN sign glowed in the murky dusk of the bar's window.

Stamping the water from his boots, Nels entered. A couple of guys in western hats, batwing chaps over worn Wranglers, and muddy boots sat at the bar. They gave him a curious inspection before turning back to their glasses of beer.

Nels crossed to one of the booths, setting his briefcase

on the floor and sliding in. Sally was already headed his way. She pulled up, cocked her head.

"Room all right?"

"Fine," he told her. "What's on the menu?"

"We got beef, elk, deer, and trout. Johnny Horizon's wild game processing plant down by the crossing does our butchering. Betty Alonzo brought in some asparagus, but it's five dollars extra, and if you want Dolly Marche's home-grown lettuce, it's two dollars."

Nels chuckled, ordered the elk steak and asparagus. "And I'll take two fingers of whatever bourbon you've got left."

Sally's eyebrow lifted before she hurried off to place the order with whoever was in the kitchen.

At that, one of the cowboys walked over, beer in hand. Maybe thirty, he stood five-eight in his water-dark boots complete with spurs. Under the chaps, the denim jeans were threadbare and held up by a use-shiny belt sporting a holstered pistol, knife, and sheathed multitool. Damp patches were drying on the shoulders of his grimy Levi jacket. The hat had seen better days.

"So, you're the governor's man?" He gestured with the half full glass.

"That's me. Nels Curley. Who are you?"

"Danny Sexton. I work around here."

"You came in with that bunch of cattle?"

That brought a widening of Sexton's mild blue eyes. "Know about that, huh? Yeah. For some damn reason, the boss, Mr. Hampton, wanted me on that drive. I guess to keep an eye on that Salva woman and make sure somebody knew how to trail cattle. Not that she needed nobody to tell her what to do."

Sexton shook his head. "Tracked our cattle about twenty miles south to a place down on Slater Creek. Thea set up on a high point above that corral where they was holding our stolen cows. There was five of 'em, and she killed them. Just like that. Never seen nothing like it. Don't think I want to again."

He extended his left arm like a rifle. "Bam. Bam. Bam. Bam. Bam. As fast as she could work the bolt on that rifle. Then we mounted up and rode down there. One of them boys was gut shot. Salva, she asks, 'You want to cap him?' And I shakes my head. So, she steps down, sort of fishes around under her slicker for that pistol. She walks up and aims real careful like, and shoots him in the head."

Sexton screwed up his face into a distasteful squint. Nels noticed for the first time that he was somewhat unsteady on his feet and wondered just how many beers the man had already chugged down.

"Me, I never seen a man killed. Sent a quiver through my guts." He swigged his beer. "And we mounted, unhooked the gate, and started hazing them cows out. That's when Salva sees the girl. She's tied up in the back of one of the old rusty stock trailers."

"What girl?" Nels asked.

Sexton wavered on his feet, blinking as if to clear his vision. "Marissa Janis. She's maybe sixteen. Her folks had a place up behind Battle Mountain where the boss wanted to build that fancy resort. Word was they'd just up and left the country after the Collapse, but there she was. Live as can be. And you can tell. She's been used bad. Salva gets down and cuts her free of them ropes, and the girl's crying and can hardly stand.

"Me, I get the cows lined out and headed out of the corral while Salva sees to the girl. I'm maybe ten minutes on the trail, pushing that bunch of mixed stuff, and Salva and the girl ride up. Salva tells me Marissa's family's dead. That in the middle of the night, riders killed her mother and father and two brothers. Took their place for their own and took Marissa for...well, you know. Then Carullo's raiders take her again. Says Marissa's been through hell, and she don't want no kind of attention from a man. And if I so much as speak to her wrong, I'll wish I hadn't."

Sexton shakes his head. "Not Mama Sexton's boy. No sir. I'd just seen Salva shoot down five men. Think I'm gonna so much as make a peep to that girl?"

"So, the three of you drove the cattle back?"

"Yep." Sexton pursed his lips, brows lowered. "Turns out, Thea Salva knows which end of a cow to push, and Marissa, she's a ranch girl, held up her end right fine. And then it started raining, and, well, what with that lightning and thunder, and the memory of them dead men staring sightlessly at the sky? Guess I don't need to do no more raiding down south of the line."

Nels considered the man. "You think Bud Carullo is going to retaliate? Send another bunch north? Turn this into an old-fashioned range war?"

"Hope not." Sexton belched. "Carullo can read sign like anybody else. Five of his hired guys are dead without knowing what hit 'em? You see, Thea Salva left a cartridge case on each of those boys she killed. Like a calling card."

"Seven-millimeter PRC," Nels supplied.

Sexton blinked as if to clear his muddled thoughts. "You know that long gun of hers? Looks like something lifted off a sniper in a combat unit. Come from some factory up at Cody. Scope's damn near as long as my arm."

Nels chewed on that as Sally brought him his bourbon. As she passed, she shot Sexton a warning look that he missed completely.

"Wonder what made Salva sign on with Dewey Hampton?" Nels sipped his bourbon. Might have been some of the last Kentucky whiskey left in the state. He figured Sally was going to charge him an arm and a leg.

"Money," Sexton insisted, tossing off the last of his beer. "Boss is paying her in cash. Only way she works." He shook his head, harder this time. "Me? I'm glad she's paid and pulling out. Job's done and good riddance. Spookier than hell, riding with that woman. Knowing that if you piss her off, you'll never know you've been killed 'til your heart's blown out, and you're on the ground dying."

Sally had stopped and muttered something to the other cowboy, followed by a jerk of her head in Sexton's direction. The cowboy shot a look over his shoulder, sighed, and rose. Walking up, he grabbed Danny Sexton by the elbow. "Sorry, old buddy, but we got to go." To Nels, he added, "Don't pay him no mind. He's drunk and making shit up. Huh, Danny? Always a wild bullshit story when the truth wasn't nothing like that."

"Bullshit?" Sexton whispered in a haunted voice. "Five guys. Bam. Bam. Bam..."

But before he could finish, his friend had shoved him out the door.

Nels rotated his glass of bourbon. Two men died when Bud Carullo stole the cattle. Five more when Dewey Hampton took them back. Night riders killed Marissa Janis's family and took her for sex, and no one raised a finger? What the hell did that mean for the border?

Sally appeared with a plate full of steak and a garnish of asparagus—if three stalks could be considered a garnish. Setting it down, she studied him through thoughtful eyes. "I wouldn't want Danny getting into trouble. Get my drift? He's a good kid. No telling what Dewey Hampton might do if catches wind that Danny'd run 'is mouth."

"Gotcha," Nels told her with a smile. "I'm here to stop trouble, not make it. Now, what's your take? These raided family ranches? Is this thing between Hampton and Carullo going to…?"

Through the window he could see two horses trotting up. The woman on the mud-spattered-and-tired gray needed no introduction. Not that she could have been mistaken, given the extra-long cased rifle tied crosswise behind her saddle: Thea Salva.

Behind her rode the rail-thin girl on a blood bay. She, too, looked exhausted, her narrow face pale under a sodden hat. Both women dismounted stiffly, tied off on one of the posts, and clumped their way to the door. Salva led the way in. The worn Bailey hat just made her that much taller. And she'd started at well over six feet. Beneath the rain-sheeted slicker, she wore a fleece-lined Levi coat, faded jeans; a large silver buckle adorned her belt. The woman's riding boots were soaked and muddy, sides scrubbed from the stirrups.

When she fixed her black eyes on Nels, a prickle ran down his back. Like looking into the eyes of a snake: cold and deadly. Somehow fitting for her high-cheeked face and the straight nose above that pinched line of her lips. Dark-brown hair hung down beneath her slicker in a ponytail. She might not have been considered beautiful, but by damn, something about her was almost magnetically attractive.

The girl behind her was half a head shorter, with brown hair. Pursed lips were framed by her delicate chin. Uncertainty reflected from her expression, something jagged and sharp in her darting hazel eyes. Water dripped from her yellow slicker.

"Sally?" Thea called in a modulated voice. "We need a room."

"Word was you were pulling out," Sally said, turning.

Thea Salva chuckled under her breath. "Tried to. Little Snake's over its banks. Low-lying roads are flooded. And wouldn't you know, Marissa and I get everything loaded in the horse trailer, start up the truck, and that big old dually just spins its tires in the mud. Either I get someone to pull me back to the asphalt with a tractor, or I'm waiting until it dries out."

"Since there's two of you, you'll need two queens." Sally glanced sidelong at Nels. "That'd be twice the usual rate."

"Got it." Salva reached into her back pocket, produced a wallet, and stripped out two twenties. "Forty bucks. There you go."

Usual rate? Nels gave Sally a scathing look as the woman avoided his eyes and hurried back of the bar for the room key.

Then, Salva's black eyes fixed on him; she stepped forward, heedless of the mud she tracked across the floor. "You're the governor's man?"

Nels shrugged, that eerie tingle still at the back of his neck. "I'm Nels Curley."

"After the trial up in Cody, Agar wanted to shoot Director Edgewater himself, but his staff talked him out of it. You part of that?"

"I was."

"I worked for Edgewater."

"I know."

Thea Salva's lips twitched. As if Nels had passed some sort of test, she said, "Just as well. Edgewater was a real piece of shit."

Nels would have smiled, but that look in Salva's black eyes kept feeding the cold quiver down in his guts. Through it all, the girl, Marissa, just watched wide-eyed, her body bunched, as if to bolt at the first sign of trouble.

Sally emerged from behind the bar, handing Thea

Salva the key. "Might be more than a night if this weather doesn't break."

"Too bad you've got such a waiting list for those rooms." Salva rattled the old-fashioned key.

With that, she turned for the door, but Nels noticed that she kept an eye on his reflection in the bar mirror. Marissa followed quietly, her wounded-bird gaze flicking this way and that.

Through the window, Nels watched them mount, cross muddy 3rd Street, and tie off in front of the hotel. They were stripping tack, carrying it into one of the downstairs rooms, when Sally walked up and sighed.

"Something about that woman always gives me the creeps."

"Yeah." Nels chewed another piece of steak. "Twenty bucks? Standard rate, huh?"

Sally bit off a sharp bark of laughter. "That's a discount I only give to people I'm afraid might kill me."

———

Nels finished his steak, having first polished off the three spears of asparagus. As he chewed the last bite, a jacked-up Ford F-350 pickup roared into the parking lot. An oversized light bar atop the truck's headlights blazed through the bar's window in a shaft of blinding white. When they went dark, he could see the big Ford was covered with chrome and rode on a six-inch lift kit. Aggressive off-road tires were muddy, and water dripped from the fenders. When the driver's door opened, a big man emerged. Silver hair poked out under a creamy white Stetson, and he wore an expensive fringed leather coat adorned with beadwork, fitted tan slacks, and gleaming custom boots. As he swung down from the cab, his coat hung for a second, exposing a chrome 1911 in a tooled-leather holster.

From the passenger and rear doors, three other men climbed down, all following the elder as he headed for the bar. Each carried a black AR-15 carbine with various gadgets attached to the Picatinny rails.

Nels felt that old sense of premonition as the man slammed the door open, scanned the room, and fixed Nels with a blue-eyed stare. The big man's boots rapped like hollow pistol shots as he crossed the floor. He drew up at Nels's table, a crooked smile on his thin lips.

"Let me guess," Nels said, rising. "You'd be Dewey Hampton."

The three guys who'd followed Hampton took surrounding positions. Two were big, muscular, and tough, even without the cut-down ARs they carried. The third was the kid from the roadblock, Rory Jackman. He gave Nels an evil glare.

"Sit down," Hampton ordered. "We need to get some things clear."

As Hampton slid into the booth across from him, Nels said, "Surprised it took you this long."

"I had some things to do." The blue eyes narrowed. "Here's the deal: Things have changed. The country's gone. We're on our own down here. Now, your boss and I got crosswise once before. Okay. I get it. But that was a different time, in a different world. Now, I don't know why you're here. But since you are, you can take a message back to your boss. The Little Snake country is ours. We don't need him poking his nose into it. *Capiche?*"

Nels's heart began to race. "The governor's already removed two petty little dictators from their supposed kingdoms. You'd be the third."

Hampton's stare turned glacial. "You better think that

through, messenger boy. I've got sixty riders at my beck and call. If you think that silly little WNG post over at Baggs is any threat, I can take them out whenever I please. What's that? Twenty guys? They'll never know what hit them. Assuming they don't just switch sides to save their skins."

"Bad idea," Nels told him. "You might have sixty riders. Agar's backed by the entire Wyoming National Guard. You'd lose against the military."

Dewey Hampton leaned back, a clever smile breaking. "Maybe in a stand-up fight. My people can slip into the backcountry. Bleed you slowly. Strike and vanish like the mist. Play Apache with hit-and-run raids. I can make the cost of taking the Little Snake country so high, it won't be worth it to Pete Agar." A pause. "Not when he can deal."

"Deal how?"

"We'll send him trade. Cattle. We've got producing natural gas and oil wells, other resources in return for refined gasoline and diesel and some other staples. Call it the price of peace." Hampton leaned back, the palms of his hands flat on the table. "And we'll run the border down here. What you call the Second Quadrant. So, part of the deal is that Sakroy and his little band of play soldiers pack up and vamoose."

"Again, I'll save you the wait." Nels leaned forward. "Pete Agar, you see, has this idealistic fixation that we're going to save civilization. We've got everything we need to keep the lights on and the refrigerators full, assuming somebody like you doesn't screw it all up. If the governor lets you set up as a sort of local feudal lord, what's to stop others?"

Hampton's smile was the sort you'd see on a hangman's face before he pulled the drop lever on the gallows.

Nels leaned back. "So, here's the governor's deal: You go back to your ranch and run your business. The Snake

River Valley remains part of Wyoming just like it always has been. Who knows, maybe they'll send you to the legislature, and you can have your vote just like everyone else." A pause. "Oh, and stop raiding ranches. After my report, I suspect that a team from the Division of Criminal Investigation will be coming to Dixon to look into those missing ranch families whose land your cattle are grazing on."

In a low voice, Hampton asked, "What makes you think you're going to report anything, messenger boy?"

Nels glanced warily at the three men surrounding the booth. During the exchange, no change of expression had crossed their faces. But, he noticed, their hands were on the pistol grips, fingers laid on the receivers just above the triggers. Rory Jackman was almost salivating, eyes burning with anticipation.

Hampton said reasonably, "You're in my world now, and my word is law." To his goons, he added, "Take him out back. One shot to the head. We'll send it off to Pete Agar in Cheyenne. Can't think of a way that good old Nels, here, could be more eloquent."

"You really don't want to start something you can't finish." Nels fought to keep his face blank while his brain was screaming.

"Uh, boss..." One of the gunmen pointed at the window.

Nels turned, seeing Thea Salva slopping across the rain-stippled puddles in the road. The long and bulky cased rifle was propped over her shoulder. The rain was battering her sodden hat.

"Hold it," Hampton said thoughtfully. "I want you guys around when she's here. Rory, go keep an eye on the hotel."

Rory made a face, started to protest, but at the look in Hampton's eye headed for the door.

The big blond goon with the mashed nose said, "The way Danny Sexton tells it, she killed those five men with not a second separating the shots."

The black-haired guy with the razor-thin nose said, "Yeah, but Danny said she's nothing without that big rifle. Said she got close and took a long time sighting before she shot that last guy in the head." He smiled. "Guess she ain't no kind of a pistolero."

"Never seen her so much as look at that big Smith she carries, but the way she cuddles that oversized long-distance rig? You'd think it was a baby."

"Boss," the blond said. "Pinky says that girl she rode in with? It's Marissa Janis. And you know what we did to her"

"Shut up!" Hampton snapped.

Thea Salva passed Rory in the doorway as he left. She took a long moment, scanning the room, gaze lingering on Hampton and his goons. Nels wasn't sure, but something seemed to change in her dark eyes. A subtle hardening. Nodding in Hampton's direction, water dribbled from her hat. Then she closed the door, tracking mud over to the bar where Sally, big-eyed and pale, waited.

"I need two meals to go." Salva braced the rifle case against the bar.

"I don't have none of those Styrofoam cartons left," Sally told her. "But I can put two plates in a paper bag."

"It'll do."

As Sally hurried off to the kitchen, Salva turned, fixing on Hampton. "I appreciate your prompt payment. Your messenger boy brought the balance. Accurate to the dollar."

"These days, five grand is a lot of money," Hampton told her. "I'm good for my word."

"Guess so," Salva said. "Heard you promised that bunch out on the Janis ranch that they'd regret crossing you." She chuckled. "But, damn, keeping Marissa for a sex toy instead of burying her in the forest with her folks? Bet you never figured that Carullo's boys were gonna steal her away. Shouldn't leave loose ends laying around like that."

Nels watched the slight reddening of Hampton's neck, saw it creep up into his cheeks.

Voice low, Hampton said, "She was always a prick tease, if you know the term. But I'll tell you what..." He reached into his fringed coat, pulling out a wallet. With a flick of the thumb, he peeled out ten hundred-dollar bills. "I'll give you an extra thousand for the girl. I'll send a tractor down and pull your rig out. You just make sure that Marissa isn't in it when you pull out."

Salva's dark gaze went flat. "Two thousand."

Incredulous, Nels watched Hampton thumb out another ten bills atop the ones lying on the table.

"What are you doing?" Nels cried. "You're *selling* that poor girl?"

"Different time, different world." Thea chuckled, walking across from the bar. At the table, she reached for the two grand. Nels caught a glimpse of Sally as she stepped out, stopped, a stricken expression on her face.

Hampton's hand whipped out, grabbing Salva by the wrist.

"Guys," he called.

Sally had vanished back into the kitchen.

The blond pressed his muzzle into her back, asking, "You ever seen what happens when a 5.56 blasts through a person's chest at close range?"

Salva had stiffened, expression strained. "Bet I know a shitload more about terminal ballistics than you do."

"Terminal...what?" The blond frowned.

"Bullet wounds, you moron," Hampton added, keeping his grip. "Now, Ms. Salva, why don't you reach in with your left hand and carefully draw out that Model 29 Smith? While you do that, Sampson, here, is going to pull your billfold out of your back pocket."

Nels, mouth dry, watched the building rage behind Thea Salva's dark eyes, her mouth hard. "I'm not wearing the revolver." She pulled her slicker wide to expose her waist. "Dewey, what the hell are you doing?"

Sampson, the black-haired, thin-nosed man, had extracted her wallet. This he tossed on the table. Then he chuckled, and ripping up Slava's shirt, exposed a thick money belt that rode tight around the woman's narrow waist. Salva's lips twitched as the man unbuckled the belt and slapped it on the table beside the wallet.

"Well, I'll be." Hampton released her wrist, picking up the thick money belt and saying, "Ms. Salva, why don't you slide in next to Mr. Curley, here. You'll both be easier to keep track of."

As she did, Nels caught her furtive glance at the cased rifle resting against the bar. Not that a bolt-action sniper rifle would have been much help in a barroom shootout.

Hampton let out a low whistle as he opened the money belt and stared at the contents. "Must be thirty thousand dollars here!"

"Thirty-five four fifty," Salva told him. "Plus the seven in the wallet."

Hampton's smile went oily. "Guess there's no need to pull your outfit out of the mud anytime soon."

"Do you know what you're doing?" Salva's flat tone sent a quiver through Nels.

Hampton leaned back, roaring laughter. "Damn right I do! I'm saving seven grand, making another thirty-five and change. If you're six-feet-under, I'm sure that the most dangerous woman in the world isn't going to shoot me through my dining room window some night. And with Curley, here, I'm sending that prick, Agar, a message he can't ignore. Call it a win all the way around." A pause. "Oh, and I make sure that little Marissa Janis doesn't tell anyone what me and the boys did to her and her family. Shame. She was a tight piece of tail right there at the beginning."

Hampton turned. "Where the hell is Sally? I'm ready for a drink."

"Haven't seen her, boss," Tommy said.

"Well, go back there and bring me a bottle of anything that looks good."

Nels glanced sidelong at Salva; the woman's lips were set and he could see the faint scar on her cheek. Nervous energy kept prickling through him on a thousand electric ant feet, but she seemed as cool as an April snow. But when he glanced up at Tommy, the man had a crazy gleam in his eyes as he tapped his thumb on the fire control of his AR-15.

"Relax, Nels, old boy." Hampton smiled. "You'll never be lonely. You and Salva, here, can share the same grave." The man winked lasciviously. "Handsome woman like her? We'll even bury you with your arms around each other."

————

Rain pattered on Sally as she slipped out the bar's back door and ducked behind the dumpster. The thing was still half full of trash. Had been since the trash truck couldn't find enough diesel. She ducked her head, running hard, and hooked around the neighboring building. Out of sight of the bar's window, she charged across the street to the motel. Bent low, she fished around in her pocket for the master keyring and stopped in the shadow of Curley's big pickup to find the right key.

In a low crouch, she eased to the door, inserted the

key, and unlocked it. The room was lit by the bedside lamps. Marissa Janis, wearing jeans and a checked flannel shirt, leaped up from the bed, eyes wide.

"Where's Thea?"

Sally stayed bent, hands braced on her knees, panting for all she was worth in an effort to catch her breath. "Gotta get more exercise. That little run damn near killed me." She looked up. "You gotta go. That Salva woman just sold you to Dewey Hampton for two grand."

Marissa's face paled, and she swallowed hard. "Thea wouldn't do that. Said she'd die before they let them hurt me again. Said she'd get me out of the country. To Casper or Laramie."

"Yeah, well, when Salva tried to take the money, Hampton grabbed her. Sampson and Tommy were holding rifles on her. Looked to me like she's gotten herself in a hell of a fix. Given what you know, what they did, they'll want you dead, too, honey. You gotta run. Now!"

Marissa closed her eyes, nodded, and started to shake. Then she blew out an unsteady breath. "C-Can't do that again. Can't let them. You check, make sure the coast is clear. Just have to get my stuff on."

Sally opened the door, peeked out the crack, and seeing the coast was clear, eased through and crouched by the front of the big Ram. Not a minute later, Marissa hurried out the door. She had on her hat, was wearing her bulky yellow rain slicker. Something about the girl's expression reminded Sally of cracked glass. The kind that could shatter into a thousand shards at the slightest bump.

"Come on," Sally hissed, bending low and scuttling for the corner of the hotel. She could hear Marissa's slicker rattling as the girl hurried after her. Reaching the corner of the motel, Sally darted around it, happy to have

Marissa hot on her heels. Was about to turn when a familiar voice called, "Well, by damn! What have we here?"

Marissa gasped, backing against the wall. Sally straightened to see Rory Jackman, a rifle half raised. Rain was beating on the kid's hat, and his smile was all victory and delight.

———

"Now, would you look at that," Sampson muttered after raising his gaze to the window. "Rory actually did something right."

Nels shifted, hating the fear winding around in his guts. How the hell could this have gone so miserably wrong? Here came Sally and Marissa Janis, both marching disconsolately across 3rd Street, and the kid from the roadblock was five steps behind them, his scoped Remington hunting rifle at the ready. Nels could see the kid's smile.

"Guess the little shit caught something after all." Hampton banged a fist on the table. "And, why, lookee there. He's got the Janis girl. That's three for three."

"What about Sally?" Tommy shifted his AR to rub a sleeve along his jaw. "Looks like she got herself caught trying to warn the girl."

"Have to deal with that," Hampton said with a sigh. "Can't take disloyalty. Not with what's at stake here. It's the fricking end of the world, and only the strong and smart are going to survive from here on out."

The door opened, a wet Sally preceding Marissa Janis into the room. Sally looked mad, miserable, and defeated. Marissa looked terrified, her head down, beads of water dripping from her misshapen hat. The girl immediately backed against the wall, eyes on the floor at her feet.

Despite the slicker wrapped around her body, Nels could see that she was shivering and tears streaked her face.

"Oh, hell," Nels said reasonably. "Let the girl go, Hampton. You and your goons have hurt her enough."

"You shut the fuck up!" Rory muttered. "I already owe you one for the roadblock, you government piece of shit!"

The kid shifted the rifle ominously in Nels's direction.

"Put that down," Hampton told him. "Now, I want you back out there. You did good work, kid. It won't be forgotten."

Rory glanced covetously at the cowering Marissa. "Maybe I could have a turn at Marissa, here? The rest of the guys say...well, you know."

"Yeah, yeah." Hampton waved him away. "You can pop your cherry, then we'll see if you got guts enough to shoot her."

Rory grinned, stepped back to give the shivering Marissa a saucy wink as he curled his hand around the Remington's barrel and slid it back and forth suggestive of sex.

Hampton shook his head. "I was never that young and dumb."

"Huh? 'Cause you're acting dumb now," Salva told him. "I worked for Director Edgewater up in the Bighorn Basin. He had it all over you when it came to logistics, weaponry, talent, local political backing, and tactical position. In the end, that governor took him down and had one of his guys put three bullets in Edgewater's heart."

She leaned forward on her elbows. "So, how about you give me half of what's in my money belt and pull my truck out of the mud. Then I'll take Marissa, head on up the road, and you and your boys pull stakes and boogie down into Colorado? You'll have what? Maybe a week's head start?"

"What the hell are you talking about?"

"I'm giving you a chance to get out with your skin, Dewey. Alive. One-time offer."

Hampton leaned back. "Maybe you haven't been paying attention. You and good old Nels, here are headed to a hole in the ground. I get it all, and you two get to feed worms for eternity."

To Sampson and Tommy, he said, "Get 'em out of here. Around the side of the building. Two shots. One to each. Then throw the bodies in the back of the truck. We'll take them back to the ranch and use the backhoe." To Rory, he added, "Keep an eye on the girl."

Hampton slid out of the booth. Looked at Sally. "I'll take care of you myself."

Sally had wilted down on the floor at Marissa's feet and sobbed softly. "Don't do that. I was just doing what I thought was right. That poor girl...what you already done to her..."

Hampton pulled his coat back, drawing his fancy 1911. He pulled the bar's door open. "Come on, get up. I don't want blood on the floor. Out there, the rain will wash it away."

"Let's go," Sampson told Salva and Nels through a grin of anticipation. "You heard the man."

Salva carefully slid out of the booth, but Nels couldn't move. The enormity of it left him paralyzed, his heart battering in his chest, his hands shaking.

"Hey," Salva said softly, reaching back to lay a hand on his arm. "It's okay. Don't fold on me now."

Something in her confident voice gave him the courage to slide out of the booth; his legs almost buckled, but Salva kept a hand on his arm as they started for the door.

Nels saw it happen. Hampton reached down to grab Sally by the hair. He was no more than a foot from the cowering Marissa. The girl—backed against the wall, tears streaking down her face—jerked her slicker back. Like a striking snake, she pushed off the wall, ripping a long Bowie knife from a sheath at her waist.

Hampton barely had time to react as Marissa drove the long blade into the man's side.

"Piece of shit!" Marissa's shrill cry filled the room. "Bastard!" Then she turned, slashing Rory across the face. The boy screamed, dropped his rifle, and staggered back, hands to his face.

Hampton staggered sideways. Tried to straighten, but Sally flipped onto her butt and kicked out with both legs. As he fell, Hampton's reflex was to pull the trigger, blasting a .45 into the floor.

"God," he cried. "Help me!"

Sampson took a step, lowering his AR, reaching a hand in his direction.

Thea Salva struck, a roundhouse kind of kick with her full weight behind it. Her mud-caked boot caught Sampson full in the crotch, slamming him backward.

As quickly, she whirled, grabbed Tommy's AR and twisted as she threw herself to one side. Off balance, she and Tommy toppled onto the table. The AR erupted in a series of deafening shots that blew chunks of downy stuffing out of the upholstery.

Nels dived to one side, scrambled to get out of the way, and slammed full into Sampson. The man howled, the AR tucked against his body as he cupped his balls. Nels grabbed the rifle, tried to rip it from the man's hands. Tugging it this way and that, they careened off chairs, crashed into tables.

Rory Jackman was screaming in horror as blood seeped between his fingers.

Sampson seemed to catch his wits, shook his head, and managed to brace himself just long enough. A foot lashed out and knocked Nels's left leg out from under him. As he fell, Sampson ripped the AR from his grasp.

"Son of a bitch!" Sampson loomed over Nels, a savage light in his eyes. He brought the AR up, centered it on Nels's chest.

God! So this is what it's like to die!

The thought echoed in Nels's head as a thrown salt-shaker bounced hard off Sampson's skull, the impact forceful enough to jiggle the man's eyes.

Sampson turned, and Nels crab-scuddled under the nearest table, heedless of the chair legs he battered out of his way.

Leaping to his feet, he stopped short. Saw Thea Salva wind up and pitch Hampton's whiskey bottle at Tommy. The man ducked, raising his AR, ready to fire. Sampson was already drawing a bead.

"Hey!" Nels bellowed, waved his hands. "Over here, you assholes! Yeah, you, you fuck heads. See me! You're a bunch of..."

Both men swung the AR's his way.

Nels threw himself flat as series of shots dug divots out of the table and thudded into the bar. He scrambled over to pull Salva's cased rifle down into his lap. Like... what the hell? Even if he could get the thing out, what was the bulky giant-scoped gun going to get him?

Well, shit. The realization hit him. Salva was out of throwing things, he was almost out of table. A sick feeling went hollow in his gut.

"Thea!" Marissa's cry filled the room.

Nels shot a look. Saw Marissa, keeping the shrieking Rory at bay with her knife. One-handed, she tugged a big Smith & Wesson revolver from inside her slicker. She gave it a toss, Salva snagged it from midair.

"Think that's gonna help?" Sampson stumbled

forward, his AR shouldered. "You can't even shoot a man in the…"

The booming shots—a staccato of cracking thunder—came faster than Nels could count. It might have been from a fully automatic. Bam. Bam. Bam. Bam.

And with each shot, a man jerked and staggered. It was over before the first guy hit the floor. Rory, hit in mid-scream, made a boneless thump, the last to fall.

Nel's ears were ringing in the sudden silence.

Then a gasp from Hampton where he lay bleeding out on the barroom floor.

Thea Salva relaxed from an isosceles hold, drew the big revolver back to a ready position.

"Word was that you didn't really know how to use a handgun," Nels said unsteadily as he climbed to his feet.

"That's a fact. Best I ever did was second place in practical competitive shooting at the Nationals. And that was with a nine-millimeter semiautomatic race gun. Shooting a forty-four mag like this, there's a lot of recoil to control."

"Right. Should have known," Nels told her, bracing on the bullet-scarred table to catch his breath.

"You okay?" Salva asked Marissa. The girl was bent down, helping to lift Sally onto her feet. She paused only long enough to give Dewey Hampton a hard kick to the head. Her muddy boot left a smear on the side of the guy's face.

"So, now what?" Salva asked as she retrieved her money belt and flipped it around her waist.

"My call," Nels told her, "is that we get into my truck and drive the eight miles down to Baggs. I think it's time Major Sakroy's little Wyoming National Guard Unit takes over here in Dixon. With Hampton dead, there's no one to question Sakroy's authority."

"What about the border?" Sally asked as she stumbled

weakly over and plopped into one of the few remaining upright chairs.

"Like you said, family and friends on both sides of the line? Might as well see what we can do about making each other's lives better."

Salva slapped a hand on Marissa's shoulder. "And you. Good job, kid. Didn't know you had it in you."

"Got to kill the monsters." Marissa just stared emotionlessly down at Dewey Hampton's dead body. "Different times, different world."

Dead Hand

A Short Story

By John D. Nesbitt

Dead Hand

A COLD WIND FROM THE NORTHWEST WAS BRINGING CLOUDS and damp air. I had a fire going in my cast-iron stove and was warming my hands after doing the afternoon chores when I heard a knock at the door. I crossed the small front room and opened the door. I stepped back at the sight of a woman with tousled hair and a flushed face, holding herself together in a coarse grey wool overcoat.

"Mr. Edson," she said. "I'm Dora Avery. I live back there." She pointed over her shoulder with her thumb.

I recognized her, though I hadn't seen her many times. "How do you do?" I said. I gave her my hand. Hers was cold. I said, "Why don't you come in and warm yourself by the fire?"

"Thank you." She stepped inside and threw back the shawl that covered her head. She had light-colored hair, pale-blue eyes, and a ruddy face.

I stood a few feet away from her in front of the stove. "What's got you out in this weather?" I asked. She lived a couple of miles away, and it looked as if she had come on foot.

"A horse has gotten out. I've got to find him. I'm afraid of what my husband will do when he gets home."

"What kind of a horse is it? What color?"

"He calls it a grey horse. It looks white to me, with specks, and a dark mane and tail."

"I can be on the lookout for him. Or is it a mare?"

"No, it's a him."

"If I see him, I'll try to pen him up, and depending on the time of day, I could even bring him over to your place."

"Thank you. I'm sorry to bother you. I don't want to take you from your own work."

"Don't worry about me. I just finished the season, and I'm thinking of what I can get done on my own place, but I've got nothing urgent." I glanced at her. Her shoes were down at the heels, and she didn't have a halter or a rope to lead the horse even if she did find him and get close to catch him. "Would you like to sit down?"

"No. I'm fine standing." She held her palms out toward the stove. "I never know when my husband's going to come home. Sometimes he stays gone for days."

I nodded. I hadn't spoken to the fellow but a few times. I had gathered that he stayed in town for days at a time, drinking and fooling around. I didn't care for the way he treated his wife, but like most people, I tried to keep out of other people's business.

"I think he's stuck on a woman in town," she blurted out. "Everything seems to have gone wrong. I think I might have to go away. I'm afraid of being alone out in the country in the winter. But I'm also afraid to be gone from the house, even for this, out looking for a horse. I'm afraid he'll come home at any time and find something to harp on me about." She sniffled and gave a half-sob.

I was afraid she would cry. I have a weakness for women when they are upset, and I had to keep myself from moving toward her and putting my arm around her or giving her a hug.

She sniffled again and blinked her eyes. "I'd better go," she said.

"Do you want me to help you get home?"

"Oh, no," she said. "I never know what he might do."

She moved toward the door, and I got ahead of her to open it. She gave me her hand. It hadn't warmed up much. "Thank you. I'm sorry to bother you."

"No trouble. I'll keep an eye out for your horse. And don't be afraid to ask for help if you need it."

"Thank you." Her face was full and flushed as she put on a smile. She lifted the shawl over her head and went out into the weather.

———

THE SKY CLEARED the next day, but the cold air stayed. We were far enough into the fall that I could expect freezing temperatures for the next four or five months. It was good weather for hanging meat. I thought about going out and getting a deer.

I also thought I would like a fresh dose of society. I felt as if the troubles of my neighbors two miles away were weighing on me. In town, everything stayed on the surface. People smiled. They wanted to sell clothing or groceries or a drink across the bar.

I cleaned up, saddled a horse, and set out for town. I passed the turnoff to the Avery place, cast a thought in that direction, and kept going.

As I rode into town from the west, I saw a man coming in on foot from the east. He had the worn, wrinkled clothes of a traveler, and he leaned on a walking stick. He carried a knapsack on his back.

I turned my horse in at the hitching rail in front of the

Silver Lake Saloon. I dismounted, tied, up, and chided myself for thinking that the man on foot might take my horse.

I went inside and let my eyes adjust to the dimmer light. The bartender knew me and set up a glass of beer. I set a quarter on the bar. He took it and left a dime and a nickel in change.

I took a drink and relaxed. A couple of glasses would not put me too late in the day, and I did not worry about riding home in the dark if it came to it. This was cattle country, and if there were any road agents, they were on the main-traveled roads.

I glanced down the bar, and my stomach tightened at the sight of a man with a shiny face, red hair, and a brown hat set back. He was wagging his head and smiling as he chatted with the man next to him. I knew the red-haired man on first glance. Jerome Avery. Husband of Dora.

The door opened with a flash of daylight, and the man I had seen in the street came in. The door closed behind him, and the light settled. He took a few steps but did not walk up to the bar. A couple of patrons glanced at him.

He took off his dust-colored hat, and still leaning on his stick, he cleared his throat. "Gentlemen," he said, "I'm a lone traveler on foot, and I'd like to know if there is a place where I can work to earn a meal."

Avery looked at the man and smiled, but he did not say anything. Another man, dressed a little better, stood back from the bar. He was wearing a tweed coat and a dark, short-brimmed hat. He had brown hair, blue eyes, rosy cheeks, and a full mustache trimmed sharp across the bottom. I recognized him as Guy Warden, a lawyer and sometimes magistrate. He held a glass of whiskey at chest level and smiled.

He said, "Stranger, your biggest danger of catching a fish is near the water. There's no work in here."

The traveler put on a smile. "I thought someone might know of work."

"People come in here to get away from work. If you're lookin' to bum some money, that's frowned upon."

"I didn't come to beg."

"That's good. Because we've got a sheriff, and he doesn't take well to vagrants. Now, if you'd like to sing for your supper—"

"Thanks. I'll be on my way." The traveler turned and headed toward the door.

I must have had an unpleasant look on my face, for Guy Warden turned to me with his jaunty tone and said, "What's wrong, Edson? Didn't you want to hire him? Or stake him to a meal?"

I said, "Maybe you'll need help some day yourself."

Warden raised his eyebrows. "Maybe I will. I hope you're there to remind me."

A couple of men near him laughed.

I drank down the rest of my beer, took my change from the bar, and walked out into the daylight. I saw the traveler shuffling away, so I took off at a quick pace to catch up with him.

He stopped and turned.

"Look here," I said. "I wasn't any part of that."

He waved his hand. "Oh, think nothing of it. I'm used to it."

"Well, it's no way to be. It looks to me like you're up against it, and if you don't mind, I'd like to offer to buy you a meal." As soon as I said it, I thought I sounded patronizing, so I said, "Come and have dinner with me."

The man's face relaxed as he smiled. "It would be bad manners of me to turn it down. Lead the way."

We went to the Cottage Café, a small establishment

that was not a cottage at all but a narrow business location built wall-to-wall with a dry goods store on one side and a hardware store on the other. Inside, I led us to the farthest table in, to stay away from the draft of the front door.

My new friend set his knapsack and hat on the chair next to him and leaned his stick against the wall. He had thinning hair, a beard that was beginning to grey, and crow's feet at his eyes, but I did not think he was much over forty.

The waiter came and took our order. We each had a bowl of beef stew with bread and butter.

"It's kind of you to do this," he said.

"I'm glad to be able to. I know those other men. I know just about everyone in town, and they've got no call to act so superior."

"Well, you've been a friend to me." The man's face creased as he smiled, and he put his hand on top of mine.

I wanted to take my hand away, but I made myself not cringe.

"My name's William Bourne," he said. He removed his hand.

"Mine is Bill Edson."

"You meet all kinds as you travel the road of life."

"That's true. I hope you're not going too far on foot in this kind of weather."

"I can go at my own pace. If I want to stop somewhere and work for a month, I can. But for the most part, I work as I go."

"That's good."

"What kind of work do you do?" he asked.

"I have a place of my own, a quarter-section. So I work on that, run a few head of stock, and try to raise food for myself. During the good weather, such as it is, I work for bigger outfits. Ranch work. Roundup."

"Oh, yeah. So you have your own place."

"A small one. Typical homestead. A hundred and sixty acres."

"Well, I feel indebted to you for this meal. I'd like to offer to do some work for you."

"Oh, no. It's nothing."

"Maybe to you, but not to me. I don't like to beg. And I'm sure you could use some help."

"Quite to the contrary. I'm one of those fellas who thinks he should do everything himself. To tell you the truth, I don't like someone else doing my work. Pride, I guess."

"Well, you know best."

I laughed. "All I know is what I think I should do."

———

I WAS glad to be home again. The morning around me was quiet as I went to work cutting up dead branches I had dragged in for firewood. Earlier in the year, the meadowlarks sang when I worked outside. Now I did not hear them. The sounds of town and steam engines and the like were miles away. Every once in a while, I heard the scree of a hawk overhead.

The weather was cold, but I was keeping warm with my saw and axe, cutting stove lengths and letting the woodpile grow.

One of the two horses in the corral nickered, and I turned to see a person approaching on foot. I recognized Dora Avery, bundled up as before and moving along at a slow pace. I paused in my work and waited for her to come near.

She had a sad air about her as she spoke. "How do you do? It looks as if I'm interrupting your work."

"Not a bad time for a break," I said. "Have you had any news of your horse?"

"He came home on his own, so I got him penned up."

"That's good." I wondered what brought her out on another cold day, but I waited for her to say something. I took off my hat, and she gave me her hand long enough for me to feel its coldness.

She said, "I came to apologize for not controlling myself very well on my earlier visit."

"I didn't see anything wrong."

"Well, I didn't feel good about it. I almost broke down crying. I think I spend too much time by myself."

I did not mention that I saw her husband in town. At least I had not seen him with a woman, so I did not have to feel that I was avoiding something like that.

"Being alone gets to me," she said. "I think some people take it better than others."

I wondered if she was interested in some kind of closeness or reassurance, but she was not very suggestive. I took a deep breath and was able to keep to myself, like before.

Silence hung in the air. I wondered if there was something she wanted to tell someone, but if there was, she let it pass. She seemed to settle.

"I just came to say I was sorry."

"No reason to feel sorry. Nothing out of the way happened. If there was some small thing I could do to help, I'd be glad to. It's good to know you've got your horse back."

"Yes, that part is good. My husband still hasn't come home, but he could at any time, so I need to go."

"Very well." I thought I sounded a bit formal.

"I hope you don't go out of your way to tell him I came by."

So she did have something more. "I won't," I said.

"He wouldn't have any reason to ask you, but if he did, I wouldn't want you to lie."

"I wouldn't do that, either."

"Thank you very much." She gave me her hand again, made a pained smile, and turned away.

"Good luck," I said.

"Thank you."

I had a hunch that there could have been more. I could have been more comforting. She might have been affectionate. She was married, but her husband had thrown all that away. Sometimes the law of nature was stronger than the law of man. There were always ways to rationalize. But I did not know her well at all. I was glad the temptation had not been any stronger, that it had not been any more difficult than it was to use good judgment. I didn't want to let myself feel too virtuous, though, because the idea did occur to me, and things could have been different.

I stayed at my work of cutting up firewood into the afternoon. The sun was moving south at this time of year, and the days were getting shorter. In the middle of the afternoon, a human form appeared on the road that led in from the main road. The person was moving at a steady pace, not halting, and he did not lean much on his walking stick. It did not take me long to recognize my recent friend, the traveler William Bourne.

At about a hundred yards out, he waved. I finished cutting the piece I was on, and I held the saw by my side as I waited. I figured he had spent the middle part of the day walking from town. Unlike my neighbor, who would cut across fields where there were no fences, he would have stuck to the roads. I hoped he did not want to stay, but it was late enough in the day that I could not quite turn him out.

When he was a few yards away, he said, "Good afternoon. Your place is right where they said it would be."

"Not hard to find."

He came to a stop. He was not breathing hard, and he was not sagging with fatigue. As before, I imagined he was not as old as he looked at first glance, and I assumed his walking kept him in good shape.

He glanced around. "Nice and peaceful here."

"The way I like it."

"Far from the madding crowd."

I nodded. I thought I had heard the expression before.

He smiled. "I must say, I still feel indebted to the kindness you showed me, and I thought it wouldn't be much to stop in and see if I could do a bit of work for you."

"That's thoughtful of you. As I mentioned yesterday, there's not much that I don't feel that I should do myself." I glanced around. "If I had a hayloft, and a piano I wanted to put up there, it would be different."

He laughed. "And there would be ways to do it, you know. Levers and counterbalances. I read of a man who moved huge objects, just for experiments."

"That's how people learn."

He laughed again. "That, and by putting their fingers on a hot stove."

I decided not to try to answer every comment of his.

He said, "I don't see any stumps to be taken out. You must have brought this wood in."

"That's right. And then I cut it at my leisure."

"As the saying goes, it warms you twice. Once when you cut it, and once when you burn it. And if you have to go out and gather it, that's a third time."

"I use a horse to drag it."

"All part of being self-reliant."

I had heard that term before as well.

"Well," he said, "you've been such a good friend to me that I have to insist on doing something. I'm sure there must be some task that you don't feel a personal attachment to. Ah." He walked past me about twenty feet and stopped at a pile of salvage lumber. "I would bet this came in on a wagon."

I caught up with him. "It did."

"And I would suggest that of all the tasks you have before you, pulling the old rusty nails out of this lumber might be something you could let go, to fall into the hands of your friend William Bourne."

"You're right," I said. "That's one thing I could let go. I would bet that it's more than a couple of hours' work, though, and I imagine you would stay over, one way or another. So why don't you rest up after your long walk, and do this in the morning?"

"It wasn't a long walk to me, and I don't want to be any trouble. I'll agree to your plan. I'll be happy to sleep in your little barn, the one without a hayloft."

"Good enough. I'll find a claw hammer, a crowbar, and a bucket for the nails. Have them ready for the morning. By the time I feed my horses this afternoon, it'll be time to start a fire to cook supper."

"The debt of another meal."

"Please don't consider it a debt. Not in the country. It comes out even all the way around."

"So it does. The custom of the country."

I thought he might have quite a fund of expressions, and again I decided not to add more comment.

————

I COOKED up a supper of salt pork with fried potatoes and onions. My guest asked me if I raised my own onions and potatoes, and I said I did.

"Oh, then I'm eating up your store," he said.

"Don't worry. I never have enough to keep me more than a couple of months, anyway."

"It's good of you to share."

He did not thank me so much as to try my patience, but at times I thought he expressed more gratitude than was necessary.

I said, "What I'd like to do is go out and find a deer."

"Oh, yes," he said. "This is good weather for it. You don't raise your own pork, I would guess."

"No, I don't. I would have to salt it and smoke it and all of that."

"A deer is good. Less cost, less work."

He let me wash the dishes with no discussion. Unlike some fellows who disappeared when it came to wash dishes, he sat by and smoked a straight-stem pipe.

I poured the dishwater at the base of a little elm tree on the west side of my shack. Inside in the lamplight, I offered him a drink of whiskey.

"I smoke one pipe a day," he said. "And if I happen to have a drink, I keep that to only one, as well."

I poured us each a couple of fingers of whiskey and put the bottle away. I thought he might say something about where he was from or where he was going, but he brought the topic around each time to me and the work on my homestead. I did not ask him questions about himself, in part because I do not like to be inquisitive, and in part because I thought it would encourage him to ask more questions of me.

———

WE WENT to work in the full light of day, having sat around for a second cup of coffee after a breakfast of hotcakes and molasses. I went back to cutting firewood while my visitor, who seemed now to be a lodger, went to work on the salvage lumber. It was not the kind of job I had to oversee. When I finished a cut and my own work went quiet, I heard the tap of the hammer, the squeak of a nail being pulled out, and sometimes the thump of the head of the crowbar on a dry piece of lumber.

I saw at midday that he was over halfway through the pile. He had kept busy but had not worked fast. I could also see that he would finish late enough to spend a second night. I took a breath and accepted what seemed unavoidable. One more night, two more meals, and I would be rid of him. I had a twinge of guilt for feeling that way, but I balanced it out by telling myself that I was doing my part to contribute to the good in the world.

———

BOURNE FOLLOWED me around as I fed and watered my horses the next morning. He made small talk and was not troublesome. We were on our way to the house when I saw three horsemen riding in from the main road.

My visitor waited with me as the men rode into the yard. I recognized the one in the middle as the sheriff, with his hat and vest and badge and tan shirt. The other two were dressed in everyday clothes with no badges in view, and I imagined they were a posse or something of that nature.

The sheriff drew himself to a stop and said, "Good morning. You're Bill Edson, aren't you?" The other two men stopped on each side of him.

"Yes, I am."

"I think you know me. I'm Sheriff Miller."

"I do."

He shifted his attention. "And can I ask you to state your name?"

"William Bourne."

"I see." The sheriff looked him over. "Do you happen to be the man who was traveling through town on foot?"

"If there was only one, I would be him."

"Well, we don't need to go any farther. We've been looking for you. We heard you headed west, and we thought we'd stop in here and see if Edson had seen you." The sheriff turned to me. "How long has he been here?"

I wondered what the cause might be. I said, "Since day before yesterday. He came in during the latter part of the afternoon, spent the night, helped me with a bit of work yesterday, spent a second night, and was about to go out on the road again as soon as I cooked up some hotcakes."

"Well, that won't be necessary."

"What won't be?"

"You fixin' him breakfast. I've got a warrant for a traveler of his description, not knowing his name, and I'll be takin' him in. I didn't know how much it would take to find him, so I got these two men to go along. I'm glad to see that our search is over already."

Bourne said, "I believe I have a right to know what the warrant is for."

"Oh, yes, you do. It's for the death of a woman."

Bourne gave him a close look. "What woman?"

"A woman named Dora Avery. She died in the house she shared with her husband, which is off the main road that leads from town to here."

I felt a lump in my throat and a tightness in my stomach.

The sheriff spoke again. "I suppose you traveled that road from town to here."

Bourne said, "Indeed I did. I walked the whole way, but I didn't leave the main road until I came to this man's place. It was my destination. And as for the woman whose name you mentioned, I never heard of her."

The sheriff turned to me. "I understood that you were friendly to him in town."

"No more than any good citizen would be," I said. "But I'm very troubled by what you said about Mrs. Avery."

The sheriff's chest went up and down. "We all are."

"Do you have an idea of when she died?"

"We think it might have been night before last. Her husband found her yesterday when he came home. He had been in town for a few days, which I confirmed."

I did not think that his use of "we" included the two riders. I imagined that the town doctor, who served as coroner, had given an estimate of the time of death. I said, "Well, Mr. Bourne was here from middle to late afternoon of that day up until now."

"I'll take your word for that, but I'm going to follow through with my current plan until I know more. It was suggested in town that this man might be a suspect, itinerant as he is."

"Well, he hasn't done anything to raise suspicion here."

"That's good to know." The sheriff looked around my little ranch yard. "Like I said, I didn't know what to expect, so I got these two men to ride along. Everything has turned out to be much simpler. I thought that if we found our man, we might put him on a horse and have someone ride double. It would be even easier at this point if you could let us have a horse. And a saddle. The county could pay you a dollar for your trouble."

"It's no trouble. And I don't mind doing my civic duty."

"Well, it's the use of your horse on the way into town, and then you would have to fetch it."

I considered the prospect. "I might as well go along now," I said. "I can pick up some groceries when I'm in town. I guess that means we postpone breakfast."

"You can stay here and eat and then catch up with us."

"No, I'll go now." I glanced at Bourne. "I guess that's the way it is. Sorry."

He put on a smile. "No need to apologize to me. You've been very hospitable. As for this other thing, I've got nothing to fear because I've got nothing to hide. I've never heard of this person, though I'm sorry she died. I'll get my bag and my stick, and I'll be ready to go in short order. And to look at it on the bright side, I won't have to walk."

———

I RODE at the rear of the small company. The sheriff rode in front, while Bourne rode in the middle with a posse member on each side. By myself, I was left to my thoughts of Dora Avery. I didn't know what to make of it. I had no idea of who would have a reason to do something to her, except her husband, and the sheriff said it was confirmed that Avery was somewhere else. I couldn't escape the feeling that Dora had been reaching out to me in some way, wanting to ask for help and keeping herself from going that far. I wondered if I should have done more, taken more initiative, but I did not know what it could have been. At the time, it seemed as if I was doing the right thing.

———

IN TOWN, I parted company with the sheriff and the others. I told him I would check with him later about the horse. He said he would leave it and his horse at the livery stable and would take the prisoner to his office. I winced at hearing Bourne referred to as a prisoner, but I could see that that was the way things were for the present.

At the general store, I asked for three pounds of bacon, five pounds of flour, two pounds of coffee, canned tomatoes, and canned peaches. I hoped the store owner did not ask me about the recent death, and I was glad he didn't.

I gathered my goods in my arms and turned to leave. I stepped aside to avoid bumping into a woman, who met my eyes for a moment and nodded.

"Good day," I said, and I walked past her.

She was a well-dressed woman with dark brown hair, grey eyes, a clear complexion, and a figure that was not unattractive. She was about forty years old, reserved, but polite. It took me a minute to place her. She was Mrs. Warden, wife of the lawyer. I wondered if she had heard the news about Mrs. Avery, and I imagined that she had.

From that thought, I took to wondering about who had suggested to the sheriff that William Bourne might be a suspect. I would not have been surprised to know that Guy Warden, with or without his group of friends, had made the suggestion.

I stowed my groceries in the saddlebags on my horse. The weather was cool and not likely to get warmer, and I did not have anything that would spoil. On the other hand, unless I wanted to open a can of peaches or tomatoes, I did not have anything I could eat, and the day was moving past noon.

I was feeling hungry when I dropped by the sheriff's office, but I had said I would check with him before I took my horse with me, and I hoped my visit would not take long.

The sheriff was seated at a pine desk with the varnish wearing off. He was not wearing a hat, and he had his head bent forward as he wrote on a sheet of paper. His hair was thinning on top. He set his pen in the ink bottle and looked up.

"Get your errands done?"

"I didn't have much to do."

"Go ahead and sit down."

I took off my hat and sat in a simple wooden chair.

The sheriff said, "I have Bourne in a cell in back, but while I have you here, I'd like to share some impressions."

I wondered how much sharing would take place, but I nodded and said, "I'll be glad to help in any way I can. I didn't know the woman very well, but I think it's a terrible thing to happen."

"It is." The sheriff sat back in his chair, took up a pencil, and set it down. "You know, the husband always has to be considered as a suspect in a case like this. But Avery has an alibi. He was drinking and sporting in town—nothing to reflect on him in a creditable way, but an alibi all the same."

I nodded again. I thought he was taking the long way around the herd, but I showed attention.

"When was the last time you saw Mrs. Avery?"

I was taken aback by the quick change, and I wondered if he did it to see my reaction. I said, "It was the day before yesterday. She had been looking for a stray horse in bad weather two days before, and she was afraid of what her husband would do. Then she came by a second time for even a shorter visit."

"What for?"

"To apologize for being a little…emotional, I guess, on her earlier visit, and for troubling me with her situation."

"Which was?"

"I don't know anything in particular, but I understood that her husband had taken an interest in a woman in town and that she, Mrs. Avery, might have to leave."

"Had you seen her very often before that?"

"Only in passing. I knew her by sight. These two short visits were the only times I had an actual conversation with her, and she didn't stay long either time. She said more than once that she was worried about her husband and what he might do."

"You've suggested that she seemed troubled."

"Yes, but I couldn't say about what–that is, nothing more definite than what I've already mentioned."

The sheriff put on a thoughtful expression, relaxed, and said, "It appears that she was expecting a child."

I almost fell out of my chair. I recovered from the jolt and realized that the sheriff was directing the conversation for whatever effect he could get.

I said, "I don't know much about those things, but it takes a while for something like that to become noticeable, doesn't it?"

"Two to three months, maybe. For a coroner, a little less. The husband says he hasn't had anything to do with her in longer than that. He says they were estranged. Not his word."

"Well, in case you're fishing for something, I worked full time for the Lightning Creek Cattle Company from early May to the end of October. I was gone all that time."

The sheriff pushed his lips out. "I wouldn't have hinted at such a thing, but I have to consider any possibility, of course, so I appreciate your coming forth. The husband says he was working on a ranch at that time, too, and he says anyone could have ridden across country at night."

"Anything is possible, I guess." I wanted to ask if the

husband suggested I might have done such a thing, but I decided not to feed the fire.

The sheriff looked straight at me. "You're sure you didn't have anything to do with her?"

"Quite sure," I said. "Not at that time, and not in the recent past when she dropped by. We kept our distance. She was bundled up in the cold, and I would not have seen any signs if I had known to look for them."

"Well, no one was going to knock her up two or three days ago, anyway."

I let the silence hang in the air a minute. "I came back to see if anyone had any further need of the horse I lent."

"No, and we thank you for it. We'll get the payment to you in a few days." He took a slow breath. "I don't know how long we can hold this fellow Bourne. He seems suspicious, being down and out and rootless, you might say, but I take your word that he was at your place at the time that the death seems to have occurred. And it seems credible that he did not know the woman." The sheriff paused. "So, after all the trouble of acquiring a warrant, I think I'm going to have to release him, but with the stipulation that he not stay around town. If you want to let him go back to your place, that's up to you, or you can just leave with both your horses."

I did not think Bourne had been treated well, and I felt that I shouldn't just walk away on him. I said, "I'll see if I can help the fellow in some small way."

The sheriff pushed himself up from his chair. "Then I'll let him go."

———

ON THE STREET, with his bundle and his stick, Bourne had a washed-out look to him.

I said, "Are you all right? Do you need something?"

"This business has taken quite a bit out of me," he said. "I'm feeling a bit shaky. I don't know how far I could walk, and I can't stay in this town. I wouldn't want to anyway. People are so inhospitable."

"You can stay at my place another day. I've still got both horses here. You can ride. But before we go, we need to get some food into you. I'm still thinking about the hotcakes I didn't get to fix this morning. Let's see about eating before we leave town."

We went to the Cottage Café, where we each had a stack of hotcakes with butter and chokecherry syrup. I wouldn't have minded having ham or bacon, but I would have had to pay for two servings, and I had to watch my money. For a moment I felt stingy, but I could see that my guest was pleased with what he had. He smiled as he ate.

"This is superb of you," he said. "I'm not going to talk any more about paying you back. But I'll remember you for this."

"I'm glad to be able to do what I can."

He sat up straight as we had a second cup of coffee. He seemed to be gaining strength, and I was not afraid of him falling off the horse or fainting at my place.

A draft of cold air blew in as the door opened. I turned to see Guy Warden closing the door behind him. He was wearing his tweed coat and short-brimmed hat. As he turned to face the interior of the café, I noticed his rosy cheeks and trimmed mustache.

With all the empty tables in the place, he took a seat at the table next to ours. For a moment I had seen him as the picture of comfort, a man secure in his own position, but he took on something of the sneer he had had a few days earlier in the saloon, the expression of someone going outside himself to mock others.

"Out of jail?" he said. He took off his hat and set it on the chair beside him.

"I wasn't in there for long," Bourne said.

"I thought you would have moved on and stayed gone when you left town the first time."

"I don't know why it should matter to you."

Warden set his mouth and leveled his eyes. "What are you doing around here, anyway?"

"What's it to you?"

I was surprised that Bourne was not being as humble and apologetic as he so often was.

"Just a person who looks out for the good of the town when strangers drift through."

"Quite civic of you. Not worried on your own account, are you? Looking over your shoulder, afraid of the dead hand of the past?"

Warden stiffened and drew up straight. "I don't know what you mean by that."

Bourne smiled. "It means that events from the past have an influence over people in the present. Hangs over them, even haunts them. Sometimes it's the sense of a past deed that follows a person, like a little goblin on his shoulder."

Warden raised his chin. "I'm not used to vagrants talking to me in that way. Go tell that to someone who carries a sense of guilt around with him."

Still calm, Bourne said, "Like the death of a servant girl in Edgerton, Iowa."

Warden's face grew hard. "I don't know who you are, but men get hurt for making insinuations. I was cleared of that thing a long time ago."

"As one would expect. A well-to-do white man and a colored servant girl."

Warden's face was flushed, and he held his mouth tight. "I don't see what you're trying to get at."

"Nothing at all," said Bourne. "You were the one who started the conversation."

"Well, if you came here to blackmail me, there's no point in it. No one has anything on me. And if you came here to tarnish my name—"

"I didn't come here for any of that. I had no interest in talking to you. You're not that important. But when you butted into our conversation, I happened to recognize you, and I wondered why you were needling me. So I asked you if you had something bothering you."

I thought the two of them were a long way from Iowa to be having a chance meeting.

Warden said, "Needling. I was doing nothing of the sort." He picked up his hat as he stood up. He put on his hat, glared, and walked out.

Bourne seemed to be coming down from his level of combat as he looked at me. "Sorry for that unpleasant interruption. I suppose we should think about going. I want to thank you for another generous act."

"As I say, glad to be able to. What do you think you will do next?"

"I think I should keep going west. If you don't mind, I could stay another night in your barn, and then I'll be no more trouble to you."

I did not want to keep telling him that it was no trouble. I said, "One more night would be all right."

———

I FELT as if I was gritting my teeth, but as time went on, I felt as if I was getting closer to my freedom. After a supper of salt pork and fried potatoes, I opened a can of peaches for the two of us. Bourne smoked his pipe while I washed the dishes, and after I tossed out the dishwater, I served two drinks of whiskey.

He seemed to be waiting for the moment. He said, "I think you're entitled to a little bit of an explanation."

I had not asked any questions because I felt that if I did, I would be showing interest and, in a way, committing myself to his case. But I did think I deserved something, not in payment for what I had done but as a way of giving me an idea of what I was caught up in and, I hoped, would be getting out of. "A little bit would be all right," I said.

He took a sip of whiskey. "I was telling the truth when I said I hadn't come here to talk to Warden. But I did come here with a purpose, and that was to talk to his wife, if she would be willing to see me."

"His wife."

"Yes. Hilda. I knew her long ago, in Iowa. She strung me out and left me waiting, then took up with him. Big mistake on her part, I thought, but I had no voice. I was left out in the dark. I'm not one to leave things hanging forever, so I took it upon myself to come here. I thought that if she wanted me to, I would forgive her." He looked at his drink.

I caught my breath. As I heard once about a fellow in his situation, he had a bad case of it.

"I didn't get a chance to talk to her, and I don't know if she even knows I'm here. At this point, I don't know if I want to go through the trouble of going back into town or whether I should give it all up for a bad deal and keep going."

It occurred to me that he was not on his way west when he stopped in at my place a couple of days earlier. I did not want to push him, but I hoped he would move on. "Where would you go?" I asked.

"Maybe to San Francisco. Something far away, something different."

It seemed to me that words came easy to him. I waited for him to say more, but he lapsed into silence.

We finished our drinks with no great hurry, and I was

picking up the glasses when I heard a knock on the door. I thought it might be the sheriff again, so I went to the door and opened it.

Dim light fell on a man in a charcoal-colored wool overcoat and a winter cap of the same color. The coat had a dyed fur collar, and the cap had fur-lined earflaps and a turned-up beak. It took me a moment to recognize the hard eyes and firm mustache of Guy Warden.

"Yes?" I said.

"Can I come in?"

"I suppose so." I stood aside and closed the door behind him.

He stood in the middle of the room, put his gloves in his coat pocket, and unbuttoned his coat. His eyes were cold, and he gave what I thought was a practiced stare at Bourne. He said, "I know who you are now. I've figured you out and why you came. Stay away from my wife, or I'll kill you."

"That's quite a threat."

"I mean it."

"That would be a change for you."

Warden frowned. "What do you mean by that?"

"I thought you were only man enough to kill women."

Rage flared on Warden's face as he reached into his coat, came out with a shiny .38, and fired two shots into William Bourne's chest.

———

MY EYES WERE heavy from being up all night, taking the news to the sheriff, moving the body to town, and telling the story again. When I was on my own and walked out into full daylight, I was worn out. The sunlight was too much. It seemed to drain my energy rather than renew it.

At the same time, my nerves were jangled. I felt that I needed to crawl into a dark place and build up my strength before I attempted to ride home.

The Silver Lake Saloon was gentle on my senses. I thought a glass of beer would be all right, as the time was getting close to the middle of the day. One drink, maybe two. Nothing strong. I needed to gather a little energy and ride home while I could.

The bartender served me a glass. I was glad he did not ask me any questions or make any comments. The first long sip did me some good, and with the second one, I felt some of the tension ebbing away. Things were settling. My eyes did not seem so heavy, but I knew I could go to sleep as soon as I got home. The first glass was not lasting long. Maybe a second, and then I would go.

The second glass was slower. My thoughts came around again to William Bourne. Even if the man was a blackmailer, which I did not think he was, he deserved some kind of justice. The man who killed him should be held accountable. I had my worries about that. By the time I left the sheriff's office the second time, Warden had been arrested and then let go, pending trial, all in a matter of hours. It helped to be a prominent citizen and a member of the legal profession.

Daylight flashed as the door opened, and Guy Warden walked in. It was not the first time in my life that I had been thinking about someone and he appeared. Warden was wearing his tweed coat and short-brimmed dark hat, and he appeared to have found time for a shave as well as a change of clothes.

He ordered a whiskey. I hoped he would ignore me, but when his drink came, he took it and moved down the bar to stand next to me.

"What did that vagrant tell you?" he asked.

I was sure he had come into the place to talk to me. I said, "Nothing."

"He said something. He stayed at your place twice, and you went to meals here in town. What did he say?"

"Nothing."

"Don't lie to me."

"Nothing that pertains to you. He talked about his travels, how he worked just enough to get by."

"Don't lie to me, or I'll knock the stuffing out of you."

I wanted to ask him if they took his gun from him, but I didn't want to antagonize him. I wanted to go home and rest. I said, "I don't have anything more to say."

"I tell you, I'll grab you by the neck and make you talk."

The bartender appeared. "Guy, we can't have anyone start trouble in here. There's been enough already. People are on edge. I'm going to ask you to take your drink down the bar and keep to yourself."

"Is that an order?"

"You know I've got to keep peace in here, and I have ways of doing it. Among them is sending for the sheriff. If you're out on bail, you don't want to go back in."

"I'm on recognizance."

"Same thing to me. I'm askin' you to move down the bar. I'll take your drink for you."

I felt things settle again, but not much. I sipped on my beer. When it was close to the bottom, the bartender set a new one in front of me.

"On the house," he said. "Sorry for the little disturbance."

"Thanks," I said. "And thanks for keeping order."

I considered drinking down my free beer and getting out while I could, but I thought it might hit me too hard in full daylight when I was on the trail home. So I drank at the same pace.

The door opened, and daylight flowed in around a silhouette. When the door closed, I saw that the new customer was Jerome Avery. As he drew up to the bar near me, the lamp from overhead cast light on his red hair and shiny face. He had his hat pushed back as I had seen it before. He was also wearing a gun belt.

He called for a whiskey, drank it down, and called for another. He had his left hand on the bar and his right hand near his gun and holster as he turned away from me and gave his attention to the man down the bar on his right.

"I heard you were here," he said.

I stood back so I could see Warden. His eyes were not so steady now as they darted from Avery to the bartender and back to Avery.

"I've got a right to have a drink in here like the next man."

"Why aren't you in jail?"

"Every man has a right to a fair trial. I'm out until mine takes place."

"Is that right."

"Yes, it is."

"Mister morality. Man of the law."

"I felt that I had to protect myself, and the good name of my wife."

"You're quite upright, aren't you?"

"I try to be."

Avery tossed his head. "You lie like a rug. That's how upright you are."

Warden's eyes narrowed. "People don't talk to me that way. Least of all, someone who slums around town. Why don't you shove it along?"

"Because I've got something to say to you."

It seemed as if time stopped for a few seconds in the

Silver Lake Saloon. I wondered if Guy Warden was fighting a losing battle to control the conversation.

His eyes moved over Avery as he said, "If someone has something to say to me, or about me, he says it to my face."

"No other way," said Avery. He wagged his head. "How about this? It's come to my attention that my wife was slippin' around with someone else when I was out workin' for wages. And this other man, a well-to-do man, had offered to help her out. Help her get out of this town. This place. The trouble was, she had something of this other man's inside of her, and his way of helping her get out was feet first."

I found it ugly that he would talk about his wife that way when it was well known that he drank and carried on.

Warden raised his head in his superior way and said, "How do you know so much about what she was up to? I didn't think you had any time to talk to her. You were so busy. And if she did do something, I would guess it was long after you did."

That was what I expected. Shift the blame. I moved farther away from the bar so I could keep an eye on both of them.

Avery said, "How did I know? I'm not as dumb as you think." He patted his chest with his left hand. "And guilt tells." He wagged his head. "She wrote me a letter, which I was to receive when she was gone. It's post-marked Cheyenne, so I imagine she sent it to someone to mail to me. I just got it. It's kind of a confession."

"I don't believe you."

"I have it right here."

"Then you'd better give it to me." Warden had reached under his tweed coat and now came out with his .38, dark and shiny.

Avery moved his left hand to draw aside his jacket as if he was going to reach for a letter, but he did not raise his right hand. He used it to draw his .45, and the two men fired almost at once. Warden lurched back and flung his arms out with the impact, and Avery slumped to the floor.

———

THE ASSISTANT COUNTY attorney was the main speaker at the inquest. His name was McManus. I guessed him to be about thirty-five years old. He had thinning light brown hair, blue eyes, a pale face, and a full midsection held in by a dark-grey suit. He began by saying, "I have a few questions, the answers to which may help us resolve the deaths of a few people in our community in the last few days. To begin with, I would like to call Mrs. Warden."

A hush fell over the small crowd as a woman in a black dress, shawl, hat, and veil made her way to the chair. After giving her oath, she faced the attorney with a calm expression.

"Will you please state your name?" the attorney asked.

"Hilda Warden."

"And you were married to the late Guy Warden, is that correct?"

"Yes, it is."

"Did you know a man named William Bourne?"

"Yes, I did."

"Could you tell us in what way you knew him?"

"He was a suitor of mine, many years ago, in Iowa."

"Would he have had any reason to come to this town to see you or to speak to you?"

"He may have."

"Did you disappoint him in that time past? That is, did you turn him down?"

"I did not quite turn him down. As I see it now, I left him waiting, for what I thought was a good reason at the time. I see now that I should have done more to resolve things. But I didn't. It was my mistake. It appears that he never let it go. Now that it's too late, I'm sorry."

"It does appear that he did not let it go. He told Mr. Edson here that he came to this town to talk to you about it." The attorney paused. "Do you think he had any knowledge of your husband's possible participation in the death of a girl named Harriet Johnson in Edgerton, Iowa?"

"No more than anyone else. There was never enough evidence in that case."

"Do you think Mr. Bourne was here to blackmail your husband?"

"No. I believe, as you say, that he wanted to talk to me one more time. That was what he was like."

"According to Mr. Edson, Mr. Bourne did taunt Mr. Warden with a reference to the case. Now, this may not seem to have a direct bearing on the case we are trying to clarify, which entails four recent deaths here, but do you think your husband could have committed that crime in Edgerton, Iowa?"

Mrs. Warden remained calm with her hands in her lap as she drew a breath. "They say a woman never really knows a man until she is married to him. I didn't think he could have done it at the time, but after I was married to him a few years, I thought he could have done something like that. Nothing concrete. Just a thousand small impressions."

"I see. Thank you. Let me proceed. As you know, Mr. Jerome Avery had a fatal dispute with Mr. Warden over a letter that Mr. Avery claimed to have on his person."

"Yes."

"The sheriff found a letter on him, bloodstained, but legible enough. It is written in the hand of the late Dora Avery. It does not name the man, but it states that Mrs. Avery had gone too far with a well-to-do man in town, and he was going to help her get out of her situation, which entailed getting out of this town or area. Now my question is, do you think your husband could have been that man? Or let me ask, do you think he was capable of something like that–becoming intimate with a woman, offering to help her out of her predicament, and then silencing her? Because that is what her husband, Jerome Avery, was alleging."

"Do I think he was capable? Do you mean in a moral as well as a physical sense?"

"Yes."

"That's asking a great deal of me, to pass judgment."

"I'm not asking you to do that. Let me put it this way. Sometimes a person says, I know Mike, or Andrew, and I don't think he would do something like that. Would you say something of that nature in regard to your late husband?"

She had a thoughtful expression behind her veil as she was silent for several seconds. At last she said, "No. I would not say that. As I review the three parts, I would not say it about any of them. I do not think he was above doing any of those three things. Are you sure the letter is in her hand?"

The attorney nodded. "Oh, yes. We found other things she had written, there in the house."

Mrs. Warden's voice softened. "I'm sorry she died. She could have gotten over it if she had had a chance."

"Thank you." The attorney faced the coroner, who was in charge of the inquest. "I hope to have brought things together, but to be a little clearer, I will emphasize something that Mr. Edson stated in testimony to the sheriff. In Mr. Bourne's second and last encounter with Mr. Warden, he made the taunt that Mr. Warden was only man enough to kill women. He put it in the plural. My thought is that his wording it in that way may have touched off Mr. Warden, just as the threat of a letter touched him off with Mr. Avery." He turned to me. "Do you have anything to add, Mr. Edson?"

"No," I said. "I think you have all put it very well." I do not know if he recognized that I was including Mrs. Warden, but from the nod she gave me, I thought she understood.

You May Also Enjoy:
Ridin' with the Pack Volume One

Step into the saddle and embark on a journey through the untamed landscapes of the American West in *Ridin' with the Pack*, a captivating anthology that pays homage to the enduring magic of Western fiction.

From the enigmatic reflections of a down-and-out fella questioning the choices he's made to an action-packed expedition in the wild expanses of the Old West, each story paints a vivid portrait of the American frontier's enduring heart.

Readers will navigate the steamy bayou as a determined young man faces unimaginable challenges to rescue a kidnapped friend, experience the seafaring odyssey of a man shanghaied on the eve of his wedding, encounter the convergence of past and present as a young bounty hunter meets his match, traverse a California hitchhiker's fateful choices as they lead him to a dark and unpredictable highway, and join a Wyoming family in the aftermath of a banking system collapse as they fight for their land and heritage amid a new dimension of uncertainty.

No matter the story, the spirit of the West is ever-present, each tale unfolding like a chapter in the grand narrative of the untamed frontier—where freedom, resilience, and the relentless pursuit of justice echo like the haunting melodies of a cowboy ballad.

Penned by a cadre of masterful storytellers, both seasoned legends and promising newcomers, *Ridin' with the Pack* is a testament to the timelessness of the Western narrative.

Ridin' with the Pack: Volume One **features Western short stories by:**

New York Times Best-Selling Author W. Michael Gear

Best-Selling Author Peter Brandvold

Best-Selling Author B.N. Rundell

Best-Selling Author L.J. Martin

Best-Selling Author Ken Pratt

Award-Winning Author John D. Nesbitt

Award-Winning Author Chris Mullen

AVAILABLE NOW

About Peter Brandvold

Peter Brandvold grew up in the great state of North Dakota in the 1960's and '70s, when television Westerns were as popular as shows about hoarders and shark tanks are now, and Western paperbacks were as popular as *Game of Thrones*.

Brandvold watched every Western series on television at the time. He grew up riding horses and herding cows on the farms of his grandfather and many friends who owned livestock.

Brandvold's imagination has always lived and will always live in the West. He is the author of over one hundred lightning-fast action Westerns under his own name and his pen name, Frank Leslie.

About Nicholas Osborn

Nicholas Osborn is a second-generation ranch owner and storyteller from the heart of deep East Texas. With a career encompassing everything from entertainment marketing to news journalism over the last decade, he has studied the craft of authentic storytelling and honed his writing throughout the years.

Nicholas's debut series aims to mythologize the pineywoods he grew up in and welcome readers to a new chapter of modern Westerns, born of the tall tales that helped shape the genre. His writing is inspired by the history of the Lone Star State, the greater United States, and the larger-than-life heroes, gunslingers, and "black hats" that gave us the myth of the west we know and love today.

Nicholas is an owner at his family's limousin cattle ranch and first-time father with his wife of over ten years. As one of multiple generations of his family working on the Red Rock Limousin Ranch, Nicholas has put his experience into words as an author with a passion to keep timeless Western culture alive and thriving for today's readers.

About Nicholas Osborn

About Kathleen O'Neal Gear

Kathleen O'Neal Gear is a *New York Times* bestselling author of fifty-seven books and a national award-winning archaeologist. The U.S. Department of the Interior has awarded her two Special Achievement awards for outstanding management of America's cultural resources.

In 2015 the United States Congress honored her with a Certificate of Special Congressional Recognition, and the California State Legislature passed Joint Member Resolution #117 saying, "The contributions of Kathleen O'Neal Gear to the fields of history, archaeology, and writing have been invaluable..."

In 2021 she received the Owen Wister Award for lifetime contributions to western literature, and in 2023 received the Frank Waters Award for "a body of work representing excellence in writing and storytelling that embodies the spirit of the American West."

About Ash Lingam

Ash Lingam was born and raised in Southern Ohio, not far from the mighty Ohio River. He had somewhat of an isolated upbringing on a family farm with his sisters. His best friends were his horse, Sugar, and his grandfather.

Born in 1886, the family patriarch grew crops, raised cattle, and doted on the young boy. At his grandfather's side, Ash learned about livestock and firearms at an early age. His grandad carried an old Colt with him at all times. It helped spawn a young boy's dreams of yesteryear.

Ash was only eight years old when his grandad taught him how to trap muskrats to prevent them from draining the farm's ponds. He gave him a double-barreled shotgun at twelve and taught him how to hunt to put food on the table.

It wasn't long before Ash was breaking horses. His spirited Tennessee Walker never allowed any other rider on her back. Together, they searched through the plowed fields in the spring, looking for Miami Indian arrowheads to add to his grandfather's ample collection.

Ash's family was among the early settlers in pre-

Revolutionary America. He has traced his lineage back to around 1746 when his ancestors immigrated from Europe to the aspiring American Colonies.

A retired marketing executive, Ash devotes his spare time to training police dogs and writing novels. He has found his niche in the Western, historical fiction, and adventure genres. With his vast vault of experience, he never runs out of sources for new stories. He has lived in eleven different countries and worked in a total of forty-six to date, Ash has written approximately 130 novels, short stories, and poems. More than one hundred of his eclectic titles help the American frontier come alive for his readers.

https://www.ashlingam.com/
Join the Lawless Waters Western Readers & Writers
Facebook Group

About V.J. Rose

Vicky J. Rose, who also writes under the pseudonyms of V. J. Rose and Easy Jackson, is the winner of two Will Rogers Medallion Awards, and runner up for the Western Writers of America Spur Awards, and the Western Fictioneer Peacemaker Awards. A former successful business owner, she graduated from a small West Texas university with a degree in journalism and a minor in history. She's also known locally for her dedicated volunteer work in preserving Texas history. Rose grew up in a small town with a wild past, full of stories about early outlaw gangs, lynchings, shootouts, and vigilantism that nurtured her love for the western genre. She strives to share that love of the Old West with her readers.

About W. Michael Gear

W. Michael Gear is the New York Times and international bestselling author of over fifty-eight novels, many of them co-authored with Kathleen O'Neal Gear.

With seventeen million copies of his work in print he is best known for the "People" series of novels written about North American Archaeology. His work has been translated into at least 29 languages. Michael has a master's degree in Anthropology, specialized in physical anthropology and forensics, and has worked as an archaeologist for over forty years.

His published work ranges in genre from prehistory, science fiction, mystery, historical, genetic thriller, and western. For twenty-eight years he and Kathleen have raised North American bison at Red Canyon Ranch and won the coveted National Producer of the Year award from the National Bison Association in 2004 and 2009. They have published over 200 articles on bison genetics, management, and history, as well as articles on writing, anthropology, historic preservation, resource utilization, and a host of other topics.

The Gears live in Cody, Wyoming, where W. Michael Gear enjoys large-caliber rifles, long-distance motorcycle touring, and the richest, darkest stout he can find.

About John D. Nesbitt

John D. Nesbitt is the author of more than forty books, including traditional Westerns, crossover Western mysteries, contemporary Western fiction, retro/noir fiction, nonfiction, and poetry. He has won the Western Writers of America Spur Award four times—twice for paperback novel, once for short story, and once for poem. He has won the Western Fictioneers Peacemaker Award twice—once for novel and once for short story. He has been a finalist for the Spur Award twice, the Peacemaker seven times, and the Will Rogers Medallion Award eight times. He has also received two creative writing fellowships with the Wyoming Arts Council—once for fiction, once for nonfiction—and he has won the fiction award four times with the Wyoming State Historical Society.

www.johndnesbitt.com

www.ingramcontent.com/pod-product-compliance
Lightning Source LLC
Chambersburg PA
CBHW010827250626
47169CB00010B/2982